CANTICLE
FOR CALYUTE

CANTICLE
FOR CALYUTE

ROBERT HALSEY

PARTRIDGE
A Penguin Random House Company

| ISBN: | Softcover | 978-1-4828-3026-2 |
| | eBook | 978-1-4828-3027-9 |

Print information available on the last page.

To order additional copies of this book, contact
Toll Free 800 101 2657 (Singapore)
Toll Free 1 800 81 7340 (Malaysia)
orders.singapore@partridgepublishing.com

www.partridgepublishing.com/singapore

CONTENTS

I dedicate this book to my loving wife, Milly, who has provided the energy, patience, the vision and inspiration.

FOREWORD

When you open to a page of a short story you stand before images of the virtual world and you become involved in it that world by interacting with the characters and the environment in which you find them and they find you.

The experience is considerably enhanced if the language is poetic and provides enjoyment and a sense of intimacy and empathy. Often the end result may well be a critical one and disturbing. Who can read "Lamp Shades And Cushion Covers" and not feel more than a little disquiet at meeting Eric Hausman, evil and unrepentant, and all that the Nazi survivor stands for prevalent still in the present world despite all that has gone before?

The author can move you subtly in an evocation of compassion for all that someone like the Egyptian taxi driver has suffered through the upheavals in his country. A tight control is exercised through the story that could have become maudlin but instead is taut and controlled so that what you feel is yours and not what the author has fobbed off on to you, which is altogether too easy and unrewarding. It makes for a genuine response that is really yours.

Some readers find it most appealing to experience the stark contrasts offered by the gentle paced dignity of "The Sirangi Player Of Sago Lane" and the brutal "The Peacock Dances Over Sinjar" with its contemporary genocidal tragedy. The actions take place in very different environments and circumstances. One soothes and the other disturbs: one gentle with a quiet dignity whilst the other violent.

The short story can be made to challenge the more serious theological questions of the day in a dramatic style that avoids the contentious dogmatic arguments. When it invests a lyricism in the words it can make the issues come alive. In that way it is questioning and demands answers to questions that have an even more urgency and threat to doctrine. Read the short story set in the Dominican island in the West Indian part of the world, "When the God of Death is The Death of God" and you will share the agony of Father Rousseau. Today this cry is becoming altogether too common all over the world.

If Father Rousseau tears at your heart so should the two Himalayan trekkers Hans and Rudi who had to make the saddest decision of their lives when they abandoned young Ursula on the bleak slopes of Kinchengunja for reasons we may never understand.

Again, like the human experience of Father Rousseau, the young German trekkers find the need to challenge our fundamental concepts about the nature of God. The short stories show how the genre can dramatically serve other needs, not merely entertain but also challenge and disturb.. "Was wirst, Gott, wenn ich sterbe?" as the poet Rilke asked many years before, and Hans and Rudi echo in the story, "Kangchenjunga" and the question remains unanswered even today.

The short story makes the reader face himself or herself in situations that can be remote from their own reality or a part of their present predicament but always it raises the self-consciousness that is both enjoyment and discovery.

I wish you both, enjoyment and discovery as you read on. This short story book, "Canticle For Calyute", is like few others that are available in today's market.

Happy reading.

Robert Halsey
2015

NAKED

A fly descended on to the cornea and moved over the white of the eye. It stared into the blue of the Nordic eye. The eye never twitched for a moment but stared out at a world that had long since faded. A corner of the eye was a tangle of red veins. It wouldn't be long before the eye would become empty hollow that stared out at nothing that could matter any more. But for now the red veins of the unseeing eyes were being endearingly inspected by the inquisitive fly that had started rubbing two legs in probable display of delight and assured it wasn't going to be interrupted.

A gust of wind disturbed some earth and deposited an ever so small load on the eye. Equally inquisitive were a thin trickle of desert ants that moved in single file across the furrowed forehead. In doing so it created a mild speculation as to what end they were checking the body out.

Here and there scattered about were tufts of grass, sharp blades that could cut into any naked flesh that had the misfortune of coming into contact with them. Not many know how such blighted vegetation managed to get this tenuous hold on life.

Something rustled in the sand near by. A sand lizard had emerged from somewhere to assess the usefulness of what had lain there some hour or so. A snaky tongue pierced the fetid air and disappeared again into the scaly interior. The tongue flickered again briefly not being satisfied at the previous analysis of the situation.

The diaphanous wings of the fly were delicately veined and gave out brief flashes of prismatic light. It jumped hurriedly up into the air as it deferred its position on the blue eye to the desert lizard that demanded right of way. The right of way was restored as the lizard moved away in disappointment of its find.

The wind again passed mildly over the terrain and in doing so it caused blond wisps of hair about the face. It threw another sprinkle of sand over the face that was partially covered by an untidy light colored stubble. Still there was no reaction.

The visible right cheek had a curious stain that was somewhat pinkish brown. It might have been a bruise. No one would ever know now. Indeterminate creatures that looked and moved like bugs moved along the naked length of the right arm. Nature had equipped them to deal with their explorations better than any other creatures currently examining the recumbent figure of the naked man.

Just why he had to be naked was quite another story. The scavengers burrowed into flesh without going too deeply into the corpse. Anyone would have seen the skin ripple on the taught surface as they moved about underneath in search of something to offer them sustenance. The body was beginning to stiffen. Rigor mortis was setting in. Maybe the visitors had noticed and wondered if they had to hurry doing what they needed to, before they left death to its own mystery.

The left hand was crushed under the weight of the body. It wasn't to be seen. The right hand would have created some curiosity. It lay outstretched fully, the palm open for anyone to examine, the fingers outstretched. It had been cut in three five centimeter lines from where the bleeding had stained the palm. No blood could be seen, not at this late hour, anyway. It suggested some defensive movement that hadn't succeeded obviously.

Above the naked corpse an odor of death was starting up as decay advanced and found expression in the gentle and playful movement of desert airs. It had a tinge of something metallic at first, long before one would need a handkerchief, or any sort of cloth really, to keep from bringing up.

The receding lip line revealed the dental line of strong teeth that were never to taste anything in future because there was never going to be a future. The desert lizard came out from under the thorax after it had burrowed down and up through the sand and out of the hard caked surface. It blinked in every direction as its head swiveled 180 degrees and then it made off without so much as another look.

The day slowly crawled through another very hot day and began to cool when the sun finally headed for the horizon. The activity of decay had set in and that of the feeding creature which became quite frenetic.

What looked like the dung beetles in South Africa ate their customary twice their body weight and would eventually reduce that of the body weight of the corpse. But that would take sometime yet till corruption rotted the flesh.

The curious vultures that had been circling now glided down and settled in. Soon their cruel hooked beaks began tearing at the remains of the flesh. That made the body move. This released the shiny metallic object from under the neck. It turned out to be a silver crucifix that tied up with that other historical one but without any promise of mythical salvation and resurrection. If that ever took place it would be without what had once been charming and romantically mischievous blue eyes which were now missing having long since been devoured by two enterprising vultures. The vultures began the pouring out in a sluggish flow the congealing blood and the contents of the stomach.

Fading light of day ended the orgy. They would return the next day with sun-up. The howling of a passing coyote helped to make up their mind as they laboriously ran with some difficulty and finally became airborne.

A light evening wind swept the littoral. It played amongst the pile of garments that lay scattered not far from the remains of the young man. It tugged at the shirt, filling the shirt and making it a billowing stocking of sorts. No human body would ever fill it again. A piece of paper was released from the shirt pocket and fled the scene becoming crazily airborne a few metres away. Its aerial dans macabre lasted a while till it disappeared in the growing dark that was descending.

No one would ever read the brief note that it carried away into oblivion where all things made by human hands were destined.

The brief note?

What did it matter now when it had been rendered inconsequential, which perhaps, to some readers of this brief narrative, says a little about our own stay on earth and how we choose to live out our lives.

All ends in fire or corruption. What remains does so in the memory of others…but only for a while. The vultures and dung beetles wait for the rest.

A Minute To Go

The barn was more than twenty years old. The wooden sides hadn't seen paint for more than half that time. Cracks were appearing along the north face. Some of the planks were beginning to warp. In its time it had served multiple purposes...once as a warehouse, once a stable, on another occasion a fowl run and there were times when it had resounded to the happy sound of music and laughter as young people danced the night away. Many a romance had flowered in its happy inviting prospect. Scattered bales of hay always exercised a wholesome welcome that was never passed up. All that seemed so long ago.

It was disused now and had been that way for some time. A musty smell testified to that. Winds rushed in through some broken window panes where only spiders had made home. A deathly silence had come to envelop the barn and the outside of the property that included a rusting tractor and a derelict farmhouse that now looked the ideal sort of place for a Steven King movie. Winds howled in its vacant interior, or so passers-by said.

A very early battered blue model Ford ute waited just outside the farmhouse in the gap between it and the barn. It was a picture of a once well-tried conveyance that longed for the rest of the junk yard. There wasn't much left for it to do now but to be the picture it conveyed. It had only fairly recently been driven in after its last run. The last driver had left it without a backward glance. Winter rains and summer winds of drought battered it. No one cared.

The day that had now arrived was a bright and sunny one that promised life and activity for the rest of the world. In the distance the highway was throbbing with movement of trucks and cars that roared by with passing life. The energy of the highway contrasted with the quietness and decay of the derelict property. It was getting warm but it would not get worse than that. After all it was only an early summer as yet, it was a day to be enjoyed.

In the barn, filtered light stole into the interior. Search lights probed the interior and dust motes stole rides on them, swirling and dancing, ignoring everything else.

A man, obviously of farming stock from the way he was dressed, looked about him and viewed a picture of defeat and failure with a dispassionate eye, or so it seemed. Everything was past its used-by date. So too was he, he felt. He didn't feel depressed but rather accepting in a quiet and imperturbable way. His pulse didn't race nor did his stomach cramp with panic. Such was the nature of life for those who had lost their purpose and feeling of renewal.

He was well past all that. His decision had been blessed by a certain strength and serenity. Now it was a time to let go, to leave. Here had once been children. Three sons and a daughter. He still saw them from where he stood as they ran in and out of the rooms. He still heard their shrill laughter and it made him smile. He heard the baser resonances of his sons when they returned from university later. One grew up to join the SAS and became a commando. He died in

Oruzgan Province, Afghanistan, in a useless war that had nothing to do with them. Why did the government have to interfere and get involved? No one he knew ever understood the insane reasons the government gave for its foreign policy.

When the tragic news was broken his world crumpled. Oruzgan.

Most Australians wouldn't be able to find the bloody place on a map. His son's widow never again visited the farm. She never forgave him who had given his life fighting for some cause she doubted he even understood, she never forgave the bloody war, she never forgave those who had sent him to die in that God-forsaken land and for some reason she felt that she couldn't forgive him, the father, who proved too weak and was helpless in the face of the same loss. And just as devastated. Somewhere in between all that happened, and which had happened far too quickly, the grief-crazed wife took off. She couldn't bear to wait the cold-eyed bank officials. She dreaded the coming foreclosure. She knew no one who could or would help. When their home was taken away from her it would be the death of her, she always said. The last the father heard was she was living with a pharmaceuticals company rep God alone knew where.

He wondered about his daughter, Julie, now a drug-taker somewhere in West Perth shacking up with other drug-dependent slaves like her. From time to time she would ring home and spoke briefly to him just to know whether he was still alive. She always hung up before he could ask her how she was, if she needed anything and where she was living. There was a rumor that she had had a baby once but soon lost the poor little thing. May be it was all for the best he thought in his helplessness. He wished he could be of some help to her.

It was time to put all that behind him now. He climbed on to a big table. It had once groaned with food and at other times with bales of corn. It had taken him an hour to throw the rope over a cross beam on the ceiling to get it exactly where he wanted it to be. He thought it was something like playing with the rope. He patiently made a loop and knotted it just as he had been once taught in his youth. He was pleased he still had the skills he had picked up as a boy scout. The noose worked a treat; his, he smiled wanly. He had placed a chair carefully in the middle of the table. The stage was set to bring the final curtain down on the tragic story.

When Dad and Mum ran the farm so many, many years ago, the barn served as a place of worship. They never were a church-going family because they did not belong to any denomination. They were not religious, but believed it was enough to live a good life. A home-spun ethics laid the foundations of what passed for a religious life. An itinerant preacher of sorts would turn up on Sundays and play his guitar and they would sing hymns and other songs, said prayers, drank beers till the day the preacher died under the wheels of a rip-roaring Big Mack truck driven by a bleary-eyed man. The barn had an undistinguished background. It had a strictly utilitarian status.

Above the table, from a rafter dangled a white cotton rope with a noose at the end. He casually looked around at what sprawled below him. He was unhurried and purposeful. He hoped the rope wouldn't break. He smiled at the thought. The years rushed in from all around in disjointed summaries of a fragmenting life. A quiet smile lingered in one or two directions and his eyes softened. The refrain of an old song swam in his memory in snatches: "Life is like a merry-go-round." He was almost tempted to hum it. Sing it he wouldn't; he never could sing a note. And then the merry-go- round comes to a halt. He gave the rope a couple of hefty tugs but it held up well. It wouldn't let him down. He smiled at the unintended pun. There wasn't much else to be done. He had carefully worded his farewell note and put it in a special envelope. It stood on the mantlepiece where it would be easily found. He smiled as he wondered who might grieve his passing. It possibly would surprise some. For a while it would be the subject of some conversation in the neighbourhood. His pub mates might drink a round to the passing of a great bloke. He hoped he had been a "great bloke" to his mates.

He carefully clambered on to the chair and worried about keeping his balance. That was ironic because his mind was anything but in balance. He placed the noose around his neck and tightened it. Nothing must go wrong now. He pulled on it briefly. It held. He gave it a few more reassuring tugs. That satisfied him.

In the doorway of the barn he noticed the arrival of a dog which showed some interest in the drama unfolding. It sat down, tongue hanging out, and his head went from side to side as his tail wagged in a friendly greeting. It wanted to play, thought the man with a sad smile. Life didn't allow for play, my friend, he whispered to the dog who thought it was an invitation to approach the table. He wagged his tale in an offer of friendship. It stood looking up at the man, softly calling out to him to come down and join him, wagging his tail as he did so. The man had never laid eyes on it before. It had meandered in from somewhere. It suddenly dawned on him he could be interrupted if the arrival of the animal heralded the likely approach of his owner. It often happened that way. For some reason he wondered how the dog would react to his sudden death. He looked down at the dog and it looked up at him. It called him playfully to join him in a game of catch-me-if-you-can. The man wanted to say goodbye to the only sign of life that shared these last moments. The game was over.

With swift resolve he kicked the chair away from under him. A bright light exploded in his eyes. A wild drumming lashed his brain that seemed to have caught fire. He struggled for breath.

It could not have lasted a minute in real time as we know it, but in biological time it was only a minute to go before he died. Then there was the end of the twitching, the kicking and the rope turning one way then another. Then slowly reversing the swinging motions. Before everything disappeared into the black vortex of death images from the past flashed through his dying mind...

...he suddenly saw a happy, laughing barefoot child at play running wild...he saw chooks pecking away hungrily in a grain trough... he saw a beautiful woman in college....she became his wife in later years.... there passed before him a young infantryman in the desert….he had leapt into a trench and bayoneted a German soldier…that was El Alamien … he saw the frightened and dying eyes of the man…he saw the blood spurting away into the sand…it was a recurring image, one he hated and feared, from World War 2 that often troubled him some nights…. or he would clearly hear his mother scream and he would look into her fading eyes as her cancer took what was left of her… a little boy ran out from behind a car …he had nearly been hit by his father on that occasion…a farmer ran about in the drought-breaking thunder storm…sadly, it had failed to save the foreclosure that destroyed life in "Oberon Downs"….just as it had also destroyed the lives of hundreds of other farmers and their families in those depression years….he heard a boys' choir singing of "Amazing Grace" growing fainter and fainter till all that was left were opening and closing lips without song…what had taken many years in earthly time took only about a minute in biological time...

> His feet spun in small circles …
> east to west then west to east…
> east to west...
> west to east...
> the circles grew smaller and smaller.

The dog sat and wondered what it had witnessed. He let out a soft whining that served as the only elegy for the suicide who now stared blankly at the animal.

This finale had taken a brief minute before returning the barn to its musty silence and the sad solitary observer.

SONG OF DANIEL

A deadly disease is spreading through the world. It is a hated and feared virus that could destroy most of the world and kill thousands of victims before it can be brought under control. Researchers say that it was first discovered in 1976 in the Ebola River in the Democratic Republic of Congo. There are some others who believe it has been around much longer, in fact, as early as the first half of the first century AD, although evidence of this is lacking. It remains a mystery why it ever came into existence or even when. The world will never be the same again. Now that it has, radical thinking is needed to contain it and if possible to eradicate it before it exceeds the horrors of the Spanish flu that killed more millions after World War 1.The world has to be united to act cooperatively to do whatever needs to be done. This will undoubtedly come at a political price like the suspension of civil liberties and what we hold as human rights and fundamental customs enshrined in what have evolved though the ages. We are all going to be severely tested to stand firm and have courage and the will to destroy it. It will demand that we re-examine some of our fundamental moral values.

As yet there are no vaccines available anywhere in the world to immunize the world against this plague. All over the world scientists are working over-time to invent something that will stop the spread of Ebola. This is what coldly clutched at the heart of America's first Ebola victim who entered the USA from the Middle East where he had worked as a medical volunteer in the refugee camps in the Bekaa Valley where there were thousands of displaced Shites who had fled ISIL raiders This was only after his turn of duty in the Democratic Republic of Congo where he first fell ill but left it unreported hoping it was only flu or else some other non-lethal illness.

At the time he had no problems, no worries, no fears for himself. Medicine Beyond Frontiers were doing a magnificent job. He had been an employee with the doctors. He was well paid. Life was hazardous and he knew that but life was well under control – or so he thought.

With a couple of business Lebanese friends, Antoinne and Rafiq, he flew to Lebanon where they were headed, their business project concluded and also having developed in Liberia and the DRC in a fear of the disease. They touched down at Rafik Hariri International Airport. The security was lax, officials quite casual about the passports and health inspections. It helped that Sesu's two Lebanese friends happened to know the men in Control. They cut past red tape. Soon they were being transported in a Mercedes taxi to the Reston Hotel where they had booked accommodation for their friend, Daniel Sesu. Daniel quickly had a shower and swallowed some pain and fever relief tablets. He splashed on some after-shave and returned to his waiting friends who wanted to show him a good time before he left for the States in a couple of days.

The song kept going through and through his head: "I am the Lord of Wind and Flame". He hummed it softly as he prepared for the evening of the big life. The words made him anxious.

The concierge ordered a taxi and they hopped in and were soon threading their way through the fancy streets of Maameltein, a suburb reeking of wealth and intrigue, where Eastern European high rollers and loaded Saudis were a common sight. The taxi unloaded the three at the famous Hamra Bar. Sesu's lower jaw fell. The opulence was only partly obliterated by the overt display of sophisticated sexual life. Beautiful Polish pole dancers with next to nothing on slithered and hung from he gold-plated poles to the sound of very loud and aggressive sexy acid rock. Lecherous suggestions poured out on them by drunks. It was after midnight that Daniel finally was glad to crash on a very comfortable bed and was lost in a restless sleep.

"..I can feel my people's pain.."

Next morning he phoned his Lebanese friends, Antoinne and Rafiq, and asked them to cancel any plans they may have had for him. He wasn't too well and would sleep the morning away till it was time to get to Rafik Hariri to catch his fight to JFK International. He thanked them for everything and promised to keep in touch till they met up in New Orleans in a couple of months. As his plane taxied along the tarmac he saw air liners from all parts of the world come gliding in beautiful landings. At the far end he saw a Swiss Air airliner taking off while a KLM already making a careful descent into its glide path way down. He took out a copy of The New York Times and separated the sheets he never usually bothered with. Then the metallic call came over for all passengers to fasten their safety belts as the plane raced down the tarmac to make its ascent.

"...I can bear my people's cry..".

The trip was uneventful. For most of the way Daniel Sesu nodded into a restful sleep. He was relieved only when the aircraft bounced smoothly on the tarmac. Home at last. It is popularly held that the home is where the heart is but this only applies to the innocent at heart. It should have taken only a half hour to clear customs and Homeland checks but things began to go wrong.

An official with rimless spectacles and an unblinking feral penetrating stare tried smiling at Daniel but all the smile did was menace him unrelentingly. He was asked why he stated he had been on a business trip to Beirut when he had also been to the Democratic Republic of Congo fairly recently. Why hadn't he mentioned the information voluntarily? It was probably only a moment's aberration because of the jet lag? This was no friendly compromising attempt meant to reassure Daniel he was in safe hands and not to worry. He was asked, nevertheless, to accompany medical inspection officials for a cautionary check up. It was a routine measure. He mas made to give the names of people he had met or touched everywhere he had been both in Africa and Asia. This went on and on and again on and Daniel felt he was walking over territory laced with landmines. This was difficult to negotiate as time slipped away. It was all so unreal and so long, long ago.

I'm the Lord of wind and flame...

One thing that seemed to have been worse affected was his recall in time.. He was made to go over the list he submitted. First a woman would come and sweetly persuade him to think hard about it and then men would come with their hard-edged and cold menacing accents and go over the recall process over and over again. He knew all about this standard cliched process killed in cheap American police dramas – good guy bad guy stuff. It made him want to laugh out loud.

Things began happening very fast. Home seemed so far away suddenly, although he was back States side. It was bizarre. He battled a slowly growing fear of incomprehension and fear. When asked, he admitted taking a commercially available flu and cold tablets. He denied he was ill of any known disease. And, yes, he admitted having worked with Medicine Beyond Frontiers out in the back waters of the Lutu countryside adjacent to the Congo Republic in the north. But it had only been for only a fortnight under world renowned French tropical diseases expert Dr Edwin Pierre La Martin. He hoped he could get him to use some of the recently tried drugs to fight ebola that his company had spent millions developing and which they believed would eliminate the disease. The drugs would initially be supplied free for a period after which it was hoped they could secure a firm order for the drug's use over the years as long as the disease was still rampant.

He must have dozed off after the intense interrogation.

I will go Lord if you want me

When he next managed he opened his eye he was terrified to discover he was in a totally different world of white overalls and the strange smell of some sort of disinfectants. If JFK International airport was hostile this was hellish where devilish figures moved on a silent operatic stage.

In a secure and isolated room where masked and fully gloved white figures moved in a dans macabre. Every now and then his mother would float by and hold out her hand to him. It was a very long time ago when he last saw her. She had passed away in a car accident when he was ten. His father had walked out of their lives a long time ago. In fact he could not recall what he looked like. He would never be able to point to him in an identity parade. The rest of his childhood was spent in the care of several foster parents. He was always seen as a moody and polite lad whose responses bordered on the tentative and suspicious uncertainty. It sometimes bordered on the fearful and withdrawn. He was gifted and worked his way into university where he studied medicine and anthropology.

It was no longer possible to distinguish day from night. That was a distinction only the human observer could make in a world meant for natural human beings able to exercise natural observations in a natural world. The chamber always had an artificial bluish sort of light. There were always moving beings seeming to be people, something like robots, moving about between machines. It was the age of electronic machines. There were no pictures hanging on any walls. There were no humanizing touches anywhere. Those who were animate moved in transparent bubbles or so it seemed to Daniel. Their voices seemed electronic sounds of communication transmitting only what the machines told them to say. He was conscious to reflect that outside and not far away there was a normal world where the sun still shone, possibly if it was still day, cars whizzed up and down taking workers to various destinations.

...the Lord of wind and rain...

There were children at play. Birds flew about wherever their instincts ordered them to. They were all wildly free to do whatever had to be done. At the end of the day they would all be headed home to evening meals waiting for their rest. The world would lose daylight which would gradually and beautifully be transformed into a gentler and restful light. And then a few hours after it would all start again while Daniel would still be prostrate with the same tubes running into different parts of his body.

Oh God, where are you in all of this? I want you here. I am in a very strange place and devils are eating me alive.

Occasionally a metalically constructed request would infiltrate his evanescent consciousness and be repeated as long as he failed to decipher the call and frame some sort of response; this would go on till it brought a team of technicians anxiously or excitedly running out to see if he was still with them.

Even whilst he was being subjected to this panic-induced panic-producing routines he could feel liquids pumped into his body in small doses. For meals it was no different. There were warm squirts and a feeling of being full. He was never allowed to feel hungry.

Daniel Sesu would suddenly see Dr Martin again dressed in a safari suit sipping piña coladas. All around him would be bodies lying about long having lost all signs of any life. Medicine Beyond Frontiers staff would drift past with a word or two with the eminent doctor. Martin was never any good as a communicator. He was an academic, very remote from reality, but with a lot of knowledge and a wealth of experience the strewn corpses may have added to in their meagre and painful ways, perhaps. This inner drug-created world would suddenly be replaced with Russian blonde pole dancers in sexually wild and suggestive routines. The music would be in some sort of ear-splitting wild crescendo that came and went.

Bubbles containing doctors came and went all the time this phenomenon lasted and Daniel wondered why they allowed the death opera to continue unabated. "Death opera"? Yes. He gradually came to accept that he was slowly dying. At first he made himself struggle to live as long as he could but his strapped body would make this hard to continue. Nevertheless it brought them running with their clip-boards and hollow sounding but indistinguishable questions. Then they would all melt away. His only visitor was his mother who stayed by his side in through his nausea and pain, through his angry singing and cursing.

Fear that had begun a time ago now grew till it began a tremble through his body. His mind was finding it hard to bring a focus to his pain. He looked wildly about his prone body. There were blue and red lights and led lights that created a life of their own. They looked looked fireflies from another world. Beeping sounds melded with other more melodious sort of echoes. He retained a power of wondering but not wonder which is more benign and beguiling. This must be what dying was about, assisting the curiosity of bubble men and women, that was, if one could distinguish one from the other.

...Lord of the wind and the flame...

There was no one in this world of wired existence of tubes and lights offering only drugs and no hope that allowed love in. He had no one with whom he really had fallen in love so that he knew he would never see a wife or fiance come wraith-like out of mists of pain and blurring life looking for or calling him back. The nearest he fearfully approached was the Spanish nurse amongst the ebola victims. He never found out her name. She probably didn't know his. She was beautiful in a world devoid of beauty unless you found beauty in a redefined sort that included fear and pain. Their eyes, in a sad and loving way, spoke for each of them. That was as far as it went. They would meet briefly during breaks for meals of rest and have a brief chat that was spoken in tenderness and longing.. They respected each other never to try touching each other. Besides, that had been strictly forbidden. There was no room for love and personal commitments and any case of a breach resulted in instant dismissal after a thorough "cleansing" had been carried out before expulsion. Everyone had to be focused on the dying and those who had died. The world outside waited in suspense, ignorance and a fate that would sweep everyone and everything into oblivion unless they won the battle for life. Sacrifices would be demanded and made.

Eventually Daniel Sesu slipped out of consciousness but his heart still beat. The time came when Daniel virtually offered what was left of him to medical research not that he consciously made himself a gift. Some drugs that needed radical application were made for the sake of research since he was virtually now dead.

..I will go, Lord...please take me away from this hell. What have I ever done to make you so cruel?...

There was no one from whom permission would be needed; there were no forms to fill in and no authority to be obtained in the usual manner. Whether we consider it was a breach of medical ethics or not, whether we consider it to have been criminally irresponsible or not what was done was a desperate attempt to find a cure or do enough to point the way to a final breakthrough.. It might provide the answer to life otherwise denied to the world. The end would justify the means and if it did not, well, Daniel Sesu was a dead man anyhow, so what could be lost? What was a philosophical quagmire might be a matrix of new life for the world.

Damn you. Where are you? What's keeping you?

One conclusion of the story was the zipping up of the body bag and bubbled workers coming in and bearing the corpse out to a waiting fully sanitized and protected truck that would take it away for disposal, whatever that may have been, wherever it may have been and however it was executed.

If millions of would-be victims could be given the choice just then as to what should be the desired outcome, we are left to wonder whether moral revulsion would decide the issue or the choice for life would prove too strong.

"The Song of Daniel" goes on unsung more often than not but finding increasing numbers of singers in pained voices all around the world, in places like Kodone, Darfur, Nigeria, and also hovered above the steaming tropical and equatorial forests to name just a few places. The singing rose above a growing mass of waving black flags like a massed choir of hell in an anthem that was being carried throughout the world.

JEAN AND JANE

So much of what I have to say about my two women I cannot because I've got neither time nor space right now. And if the truth must be known neither the inclination. We have enjoyed a platonic situation for many years. Jean and Jane's situation was different, one I shan't go into, they being friends of mine. What I am going to say, however, may sound ridiculous, but it isn't. So much that will be left unsaid will remain just as ridiculous because I have to remove as much as possible of myself from the story. It's their story, after all. It is a story I got from Jane. I got the story from Jane afterwards when she had become composed and felt up to it. It took a long time for me to understand it. It was just too ridiculous the more I think about it. I'll leave you to make up your own mind. But on with the actual story.

Jean and Jane were such lovely people, well into their seventies, both bespectacled and angular spinsters by conventional standards. By that I mean they were an aging lesbian couple who had made their commitments to each other many years ago, long before it became fashionable for lesbian women to come out of their respective cupboards. They had lived quietly and with sobriety and commendable decorum.

Jane was an artist, to use an euphemism. She loved painting and sketching. She did a sketch of me once which threatened our relationship till she got rid of it. I thought it was a subtle sort of getting even with me over an argument we had once got into about art. Her many canvases declared more passion than ability.

Jean had always been a wheezy and sniffy primary school teacher who retired on a decent superannuation and that with a part pension enabled her to live comfortably in retirement. She was an avid reader of socialist literature, and a strong supporter of the under-privileged and working class people, many of whom she was known to help from time to time as far as she could afford to.

She never failed to work on my dubious socialist sympathies. I can take it or leave it. You could never get me to the barricades. Never.

As age advanced upon her she developed a weak heart. A couple of angioplasties later and within a short interval of each other had weakened her. It had made her a very anxious person who at times brought on her attacks. That was what happened when she and Jane decided one night that they would go to the State Theatre's offering of Ibsen's "Hedda Gabler" which was held on the sixth floor. After the show they had stayed behind to have a couple of drinks with some friends with whom they had come out for the show. Then it was time they went home so they took their leave happily and got into a lift that had quickly and unaccountably got near to capacity. They were right at the back. Jean soon realized it was all a most unfortunate decision because they came to share the lift with some rather loud and inclined to be loutish younger set of theatre goers who were not averse to putting on a show of their own, lacking refinement and more than a bit coarse. Then it happened.

The stink was unbearable. Someone's guts were rotten. A sly fart had brought tears to the eyes of the ladies and oaths from the men.

How does one deal with such a situation on such a social occasion that earlier happened to promise so much but now ended miserably. One could hardly call for the culprit to confess by raising his or her hand. There was a bustling about as attempts were made to shift one's position to get as far from the stench of rotting cheese, but where could anyone shift to? There was no escape. Some gagged and some swore threats at the offender and much more, if he or she were caught. But how does one catch a farter in a lift?

Jane had got into an argument with someone she openly accused. Clearly the worst option. What followed was a deafening denial and more that can't be reported here. Calm and clear thinking would have helped. Like suggesting to halt the lift's creaking descent, but the lift was so crowded it wasn't possible without accidentally groping someone. That would have added another dimension to the anarchy. It was really a ridiculous situation as anyone caught up in such a situation would soon discover.

Then it happened. Jean gave a high pitched sort of cry and clutched her heart. Jane who was nearest cried out in alarm, knowing of Jean's on-going heart problem. The lift came to a jolting halt and everyone clutching at their noses made for the open door. Only the more adult and mature realized the present drama that was unfolding as a tragedy. They had just vicariously witnessed the illusionary one of poor Hedda Gabler to be suddenly drawn to the real-life situation that was threatening to be more real.

A sort of progression from one tragedy to another in such a short period of time. Or is life meant to be dark comedy of manners? Immediately mobile phones were whipped out as the emergency number was punched out in panic and fear. Someone knelt by the prone Jean and felt her pulse. Another called for CPR to be administered. Everyone had some idea what should be done but no one moved to do anything. Jane kept wringing her hands and calling fort help.

This is life. The ridiculous comic inextricably mixed with the deadly serious. A ying and yang situation, a sort of social paradox. A mixture of the tragic vision and bathos. Life is a stage and we are all its players who strut and fret our daily hour or two upon it and then wait the next act. But not for poor Jean who is no longer part of a ying or yang, or anything for that matter.

Jane who later related the entire episode said she phoned me as soon as she could. At first I could make nothing of her hysterical babble. I told her something ridiculous like "You've been drinking too much again, Jane. Please put Jean on the line please. I'll speak to her." It made for a terrible irony but what was I to do, I who could not comprehend all that was unfolding? That a fart could blow one away for ever. In a hideous moment I contemplated what an appropriate headstone for Jean might read, but cursed myself for such opportunistic crassness. Most unworthy of me. And I do love poor Jean, after all.

KANGCHENJUNGA

Kangchenjunga is rock and ice. Kangchenjunga dominates everything. Pandim. Kabru. Talung. Everything. It does not share in life and death.It is beyond everything.

From anywhere the massif of rock and ice can be seen on a clear day. Look up from any street, look out from any north face window in Darjeeling and it is there, ascendant and remote. What strength! What power! No wonder the mountain has been worshipped. In its shadow one feels the cold, indifferent indictment of the mountain, cosmic spaces and the chill of our littleness and insignificance. One feels a certain humility and the mountain's transcendence and magnificence.

Up there brooded an indifference to man's adulation and devotions: it seems to menace by its indifference. The Darjeeling late afternoon was clean, crisp and cold. Yesterday's maximum had barely reached 10 degrees and that only briefly before plunging sharply into negative territory before sunset. In the market they were saying snowfall was near. We had been drinking my Glen Livet when I heard a crashing of burning logs in the grate behind me. Someone got up and stoked the grate. I stood at the window, mesmerized by the mountain, struggling with something akin to guilt and confusion. I heard Deju say something to Dr Carr. I had met the two three weeks ago for the first time.

All that I knew about Dr Carr was that he was with CARE and had been down from Gangtok many times. Deju was a local lapcha who claimed he too had been to Gangtok many times. It had been a chance meeting that had brought us together at the Oberoi Everest for dinner one night.

Deju was an enigma. I never found out how Carr ever came to know him and Carr never said. I'm told that his type is common enough, the type of westernized Indian who finds the company of European tourists congenial, but not for baksheesh, money that is often demanded with a whine. His background suggested if not wealth a certain sufficiency as with his education. I knew nothing about him except that he was always preaching a brand of separatism. That one day would land him in trouble with the Indian security. There was a curious increase in the political unrest that was starting up in these eastern hills regions. I hoped he wouldn't get some unwary tourists trapped in open sedition. I let Deju know I wasn't interested in any way with the political destinies of these people. Nor was Carr, who shut him up no sooner than he started. It didn't deter Deju who today was ranting on about his people, the lapchas, who had neither cultural nor political sympathies with Indians. I heard Carr rumble something inaudible by reply. The majesty of Kangchenzonga rendered void any attractions we might have had for issues of justice and self-determination. It had seen it all before.

An Ambassador taxi groaned up the steep drive and two well-dressed Indians got out. It was clear that they weren't hills people. Hills people and Indians over the years had come to tolerate each other to keep the peace. The new arrivals were given rooms adjacent to ours. They ran up the steps, stamping and blowing their hands as they went in. A door slammed and the Ambassador pulled away.

"No. No.We can't take it any more, I tell you. We are not Indians. Look at me. Do I even look Indian?" he urged us, leaning into our faces. Dr Carr chuckled and let out a stream of pipe tobacco smoke. Through the slight haze of bluish smoke he remonstrated lightly that you can't tell an Indian by what he looks like. Nor anyone else for that matter. Deju complained that the matter deserved more serious attention than Carr was prepared to offer. Deju's sino features blazed with revolutionary ardor.

"You British are really responsible for everything. For the mess we are in and you do not seem to care. You lot sold us out," he said.

"Sold you out, did we?" sighed Carr.

I was keeping well out of this. I was getting quite tired of Deju by this time.

Outside two Nepalese urchins threw gravel at each other and raced away jabbering excitedly.

"Yes, sure you did. Why didn't you restore our lands to us? Why didn't you return us our autonomy? You claimed to be applying the principle of self-determination. So Kashmir was returned to a single Hindu family although you knew it had over 90% Muslim population. And over here Nagas, Lapchas and Mizo were handed over from one overlordship to another and New Delhi became our capital by force. We went from one form of slavery to another. You couldn't get out of India quick enough – so-so you merely…"

Deju threw his hands up into the air and paced the floor in the finest theatrical tradition. I caught all of his act in the reflection of the window panes. This was the direct benefit of my Glen Livet.Outside a heavy mist was rolling down the sides of the mountain, obscuring the village, and poured through the clusters of pines and firs obscuring shanties perched precariously at the edges of precipices. The golden dome of the Buddhist monastery blinked before it too disappeared. I inhaled deeply. Peanuts being roasted on charcoal. The vents in the roof brought the delicious smell in. The vendors would be still bent over their earthen stoves earnestly engaged plying their business. I finished the last of my whiskey and fell into a dream-like trance.

* * * * *

The monkey temple. I was back in my guilt. From the moment I stepped into the ruined temple and set my eyes on her I knew that she was desperately ill. She lay in a plastic sleeping bag with a cotton blanket thrown over her in a pathetic attempt to keep her warm. The contents of her back pack lay scattered about. A camera here, a diary there there. A book near by. I picked it up. Rilke! Her blond hair was matted with the heavy sweat of a wasting fever. Her breathing was very labored. She was so small. She looked to be no more than an adolescent. I saw fear in her eyes as she saw me. She moaned.Near her lay a syringe.

* * * * *

"Deju, I can sympathize with you. I really can. Believe me. I am not taking you lightly at all. One cannot work six years in India for CARE and not notice certain things. But look, my work is with children. I really have no politics in India. I cannot. My work takes me to Darjeeling, Gangtok, NEFA and Dhaka. So, yes, I see things. I feel things but I have my work, too."

Deju shrugged, lit another cigarette and smoked silently for a while."O.K," he said finally. Just that and nothing more. I can't say why it did but the ensuing silence made me turn around and face them. I made a great show of rubbing my hands together enthusiastically. I said, "I've got a great idea. Why don't we get something to eat. It's nearly twelve. The food is excellent at the Oberoi Everest."

Dr Carr agreed, more to get away from Deju's hectoring and histrionics than from any real hunger pangs. He knocked his pipe against the grate and cleaned the bowl of his pipe. The mood had changed. On our way there Deju gave us some very entertaining highlights of last summer at the Oberoi Everest which never failed to attract only wealthy tourists most of whom were Germans.Lunch turned out to be a quiet affair. Hunger not politics took our attention. They serve a very good briyani here. The salads were also a treat. Coffee was from a surprising Indian blend. It was thoroughly satisfying.

* * * * * *

Come to think of it now, the morning that I left, Shenju-La had been freezing. I had to blow repeatedly on my gloves to keep me warmer. I tried stamping to keep the cold from my feet. The sky had lightened very gradually; dawn made a belated and reluctant entry. Suddenly from somewhere a woman's shrill scream of anger shattered the early morning silence. I looked around the clearing in the forest trying to determine what was happening and to whom, but there was nothing I could discern. The world had been returned to its eerie silence.

A pink fringe slowly poured over the shoulders of the mountains, none higher and more magnificent than Kangchenzonga. It was stunningly beautiful.

The sun's rays gradually reached the lower heights and penetrated into the valleys and lit up the villages from where wood fires from cottages were already pouring out. I checked out my packs and got into my jeep and headed off to the Sikkim border. Recollections of that day still bring up the chill I felt then. Once past the tea estates the roads deteriorated rapidly because of ongoing neglect.

In some places on the shoulders of the mountains there was no road and the rear wheels of the jeep spun wildly and frighteningly in the air. The scree fell away noisily into the gorges of swiftly flowing streams and rivers. I bounced about crazily, my heart in my mouth and my lungs bursting with fear.

I eventually came to a small village where I managed to terrify some poultry out of my way. I now knew that Shenju-La wasn't very far off. I usually spent a little time in the ruined temple if the weather wasn't bad just to rest up a bit as I did that day. It gave me three canvases and a meditation.I like to come here at least once a year. Anyone who has experienced Kangchenzonga just once is forever a slave to it. But that day sadly there was something more to it than that mountain's uncompromising grandeur.

* * * * *

Dr Carr had a mole on his upper right lip I hadn't noticed before. It became a part of the ironic smile he awarded Deju's political jibes. Deju had made himself, uninvited, a regular at the table whenever we had meals. We didn't really mind but he had taken it all for granted. At times he had kindly insisted and settled the account much to our delight.

"Hardstaff, I don't suppose you know any of these Germans around the place, do you?" asked Carr and almost floored me. I froze involuntarily."No. Ofcourse not. I can't imagine whatever made you ask such a strange question, Carr," I replied, a bit aggrieved and but a lot more surprised. Carr gave one of his grunts and let it slide.I pointed out I usually pass some fifty or sixty of them after I passed Ghoom when I was on the approaches to Darjeeling. They came in large numbers every year. The ones he was referring to were a motley lot of back packers, the men invariably bearded. The more affluent rode sherpa cabs in and around the place and stayed in the better class hotels. The women were mostly blondes with wild scruffy hair. They all smoked pot whenever they felt the need to. You could smell it off them. Somehow, Ursula George was different. I'm not quite sure in what way. I think about her often.Now my breath had returned and I felt relieved."Actually, I am sort of acquainted with one or two. But I can't say I know them," I replied shortly. "More out of curiosity than anything. There was an ornithologist out from Munich. I have a problem remembering German names. Anyway, we're all transients here. One never comes to know anyone in the short time one has. Here today and so on and so forth. Besides, how well do we know each other for that matter?"

"Quite," responded Carr quickly. "Come on, Hardstaff, let's get down to the foreigners' registration office this morning, seeing we both have to be leaving. These areas are under military control, remember."

We trudged down to the tent where soldiers stood about without looking particularly menacing. They cradled their rifles and looked about them.

"By he way, Carr, why the interest in German tourists?"

"Oh well, nothing really. It's just that the police were inquiring after some young German woman who seems to have gone missing," he replied indifferently. Before setting off he lit up his pipe and puffed lustily.We hung about the registration office tent waiting to be called up. A sentry looked us up and down and looked suspiciously at us. I smiled at him trying to appear friendly and disarm any fears. It didn't seem to work. Eventually Deju spoke to him in his own language. That did the trick. The sentry looked into the tent and shouted something to someone. A heavily mustachioed Nepalese officer came out with a steaming cup of tea and stared at us. We got our turn at last. We were impressed at how successful Deju apparently had been and we thanked him profusely.On entering the tent we saw a large Indian flag. It formed the background to a table that was smothered with sheets of paper in a disorderly pile up. On one side of the table was a petromax light and on the other a field telephone.

Two officers got together and scrutinized what must have been some photographs of us and then looked searchingly at us a couple of times. We were glad we passed muster eventually. Our authorization papers were in order and duly signed and thunderously stamped and given to us.By the time all security had been put in place we noticed it we had begun losing light. I had to make my move now. I suddenly stopped. Carr and Deju who had gone ahead stopped and looked back. Carr asked what was wrong.

"I say, Winston, I wonder if you can do me a favour," I began. I hoped I didn't sound desperate or in need of assistance. I didn't want to arouse any suspicion..

"Yes. Yes, of course," he replied, a bit puzzled. "Anything wrong?"

"Wrong? No. I thought I'd take a few shots of the view here and catch up a little later. And, also, a few loose ends to see to before I finally leave here.

I hope you guys don't mind. We'll meet at Teesta in a day or two. How's that?" I said.

"Regular man of mystery, is our Hardstaff, eh," laughed Carr. "Yeah, sure. There's no rush. Should be OK. We could in a few days too," said Carr.

"No, please."

I had undoubtedly created a mystery and couldn't handle it now. Carr blinked and removed his pipe from his mouth. He and Deju looked at each other for a few moments that took an eternity it seemed.

"Please," I beseeched them firmly.

"OK, then I will go along with the good doctor," said Deju.

"Yes. That's OK with me. Yes. All right then. Take care. We'll carry on."

Deju nodded enthusiastically.

"When ever you are ready to we'll meet up at Teesta like you said.OK? Near the bridge. Be sure to get there before sundown. Right?

It suited me fine. I was greatly relieved everything had gone well. I assured them I would meet them at Teesta by sundown, if not earlier. With that we parted company. I watched them go before I felt safe to do what I felt I had to. This could be seen as an act of deception, I suppose. What worried me a bit was that I felt no real remorse. It was just something I had to do. I recalled how I first met this helpless young German woman who looked to be a little more than an adolescent. This was when I first met Ursula George.

She had been running a high temperature as she lay sweating in the ruins of the temple that was overrun by creepers and plants. Up there at about 8000 metres above sea level lay a human being deserted, alone and close to death. And that magnificent mountain exhibiting nothing more than a granite-like indifference. Life didn't matter to the mountain. What was even worse was that it seemed her friends shared that indifference.

I must admit that despite our leave-taking I had no intentions of meeting up with Deju and Dr Carr at Teesta. I had lied. My meeting with the German woman had created a strange "bonding", if I could call it that. I had no idea where to go with that now.

I knew that Carr could not wait up for me at Teesta; not for more than a day at the most. He had a CARE conference to attend. He would need to drive down to Siliguri as soon as possible to meet the other delegates attending the meeting. That left Deju who could be relied on to attach himself to some other interesting foreigners with whom to spend time.

And so it was I felt no guilt as my jeep bucked and groaned up the bridle path to Shenju-la and the ruins of the monkey temple. I wondered what I would find. I could not, try as I might, get that fevered face out of my mind. The mystery of her fate moved me deeply. What was a dying German, so young, doing alone on a slope of the gigantic Kangchenzonga? There could not be a simple solution. The awful agonized groaning, the fetid darkness of the ruins and its smell.

The shoulder of Kengchenzonga fell away sharply as the jeep negotiated its final stage of the journey. Snow had fallen: the first snows of winter which as yet lay thinly over the earth in accumulations, not able to completely conceal the undergrowth.

This was the land of the Rung-nyo-ung-dut, the demon who trapped people with its invisible chains. The people died soon after that, but were allowed to roam amongst the living. The living presence of the myth was manifest by the sound of its breathing; the flitting shadows, and muted echoes one heard rolling in the valleys below. The natives believe that the forests are teeming with demons. Perhaps it is the distances and the vastness of Kangchenjunga that feeds our fears. Most of us would find it impossible to believe all that but skepticism has been known to wilt under the energies generated by such experiences.

The huge massif of rock and ice dominates everything and everyone, every thought which becomes nothing but a clouded perception. Against it nothing matters. It is totally indifferent to the fate of man. Occasionally from the peak there would come rumblings that ran from peak to peak like thunder. Pandim, Kabru, and Talang exchanged whispers from time to time. Here were living elements of pre-history preserved in the language of Kangchenzonga translated into local folklore.

* * * * *

I stopped the jeep, yanked up the handbrake and got out. A fine drizzle like a gentle spray was gently blowing about. It was freezing. Snow was imminent. I couldn't stay long. The bridle paths become coated with a fine ice and always proved very dangerous. I climbed over a ruined wall over which briars were sprawling. I slipped over a boulder and sent an empty can of Hahn clanging down the slope. I stiffened and looked about me expecting to be detected by any man, beast or angry demon to confront this intrusion. Nothing happened.

Soon after I felt the hard-beaked Rung-nyo-ung-dutt somewhere near at hand but invisible. I believed that if I found the demon I would find Ursula George. In the ruins the damp smell closed in on me like a palpable presence. The cold wind that had whipped up had died down. Now and then I heard a tuneless whistle start up and die away in the pine tops. I took out a pocket torch and turned it on. I looked around.

Nothing.

I spent some time exploring the ruins hoping to find some evidence she had been here – anything, passport, beads, an airline ticket, diary - anything that could link me to her. It's as though she had never existed and yet I think I caught the stench of her fever. I sat down. No, there was no imagining it. It made me shake my head. She could not have left the place by herself. I doubted that she could have lived another twenty four hours alone. Could her friends have returned for her? I asked myself. If they hadn't then who could have removed her? I wondered if she lay dead somewhere in the forest. I came out of the ruined temple and scouted around in a hundred metre radius. Neither soil nor vegetation had been disturbed. High up from the storm-covered summit came a strange sort of cry.

"Was wirst du tun, Gott, wenn ich sterbe?"

What, indeed, God, would you do if I died? What God always says?

Nothing.

Or was it the Rung-nyo-ung-dutt?

Then I found her. She was all alone. Suddenly the cave yielded her up to the world. I thought this must be an hallucination.Yet it was too real.It couldnt have been. We were back in the cave. How was this? Was I dead? What was happening to me?

This is all there is. This is all there has always been. Nothing more.There was no reply. Her eyes were shut. She was really burning up. She needed urgent medical attention but there were no telephones on the rugged and forested slopes of this mountain. Communication was impossible. Her tongue kept snaking out of her parched lips. Her tiny fists were clenched.

"Rudi," she kept calling, and something else which I couldn't quite catch.

"Rudi? Wo bist du? Bitte sag mir." She wanted to know where he was

"Rudi?" I asked, wanting some more information about who he was.

"Du bist gegangen Du bist gegangen?" she called softly, again and again.

She was close to death. Her breathing was a gurgle at times. I could almost feel the heat from her body.

The interior smelt of decay. All around was darkness, within and outside. In the innermost core was a small black straining phallic core where dead flowers lay, a sad touch of irony. Here sprawled poor Ursula George. None of this made any sense. Maybe this was life. None of it made sense unless what you made of it. Language was made to make some sense of the inscrutable if the imagination was able to invent this reality.

"Was wirst, Gott, wenn ich sterbe?" -she quoted from Rilke.

Through the ages this has been a question that God has never answered.

* * * * *

I left her to the protection of the temple. A dying woman not very much more than an adolescent had been abandoned here to die a horrible death at the base of Kandchenzonga and its icy winds. I took refuge in my jeep where I tried to hide myself from the moral squalor. I was glad in a way to slip behind the steering wheel to feel a measure of control over something within my capabilities, something I could understand and direct. I rejoiced in the surge of energy. I felt revitalized. Its shuddering start returned me to the land of the living.

The drive down to Bagdogra airport later in the day was mercifully uneventful. After I had retrieved the special case containing my three canvasses from the jeep, I engaged a sherpa driver to return the jeep to Sikkim, but only after we had shared a meal and a hot, steaming cup of tea. The sherpa was an opportunist who talked in broken English all the time. I got to know all about his family who dealt in jade and furs. He could supply me all the jade I wanted. New furs were being smuggled out of Tibet every day. His brother was a supplier who would be happy to let me have some at a reasonable cost. I politely fended off all his offers and we parted company the best of friends after I slipped him some extra money as a friendly gesture.

After the jeep had noisily tooted a farewell and disappeared behind a cloud of dust, I took myself down to the customs and immigration check-out point. Once within the comparative shelter of the transit lounge and from strong winds, aggressive coolies and cadaverous beggars demanding bakshees desperately to get some food, I found a seat and sat down and closed my eyes to relax and let the stress out of my system. What I could not succeed in doing more than anything else was to disengage from this reality, and also to get Ursula out of my mind. I began to feel responsible for her. Later, after I felt a bit better I scouted around and found a newsstand and bought a paper. It was then that I became aware of two young bearded Germans. Their back packs and bedrolls lay on the floor between their feet. What drew me to them as I watched from a short distance was the hurt of their silence.

Each seemed a spirit-less shell. Their eyes were fixed on the floor; as if they were searching a secret pattern in the mosaic. I went over to the Air India counter and handed over my luggage. The small transit lounge was now filling up and alive with passengers on the move. They were accompanied by all the usual throng of well-wishers to see them off. They were getting quite noisy. My manoeuvres had brought me surreptitiously near to the forlorn couple and I heard one ask the other,

"Rudi, hilf mir – hilf mir, bitte..." one said. He was clearly troubled and struggled with guilt.

I lost the rest in a sudden flare up of conversation near me. I cursed the lot under my breath. Hans whispered something very gently under great strain. They picked up some belongings and moved along with the throng of pushing passengers. They picked up their luggage and began moving along to the exit as a metallic voice called for all passengers flying to New Delhi to board the aircraft. They passed close to me.

I heard Rudi mumble to himself quite dramatically as if reciting something he recalled, "Was wirt du tun, Gott, ich bin bange." His heart and mind were overloaded in angst as he made his confession to his secret God. Suddenly there was a barrier of multicolored saris between them and me as the women pushed past. The two Germans had increased the distance between us.

I quietly called out, "Hans."

I wanted to know him. To find out about Ursula George. To let them know, in fact, that I knew about their secret.

The blonde, the taller and what appeared as the gentler, the almost effeminate, turned in fear and looked about him. He looked into faces about him furtively. He looked back a couple of times and said something to the other man who decided to ignore him. I thought I saw both fear, guilt and what passed for suffering.

Once I felt the shuddering, trundling wheels of the airbus as it roared under me, I gave my attention to "The Times of India". Only once did I look out of the port side window. Below me, standing out in magnificent dramatic show lay the Himalayan arc. Indifferent to life and death and everything human.

I got to know Rudi and Hans at Palam airport in New Delhi. I asked if I could join them at their table for coffee and something to eat. They were cautiously obliging with faint welcoming smiles one extends to strangers under such circumstances. We discussed Sikkim and the weather and other things but they weren't too keen to open up on trekking and reticent about Ursula George when I turned the conversation around to her. They were shocked at how much I knew about her. Hans blinked several time, visibly moved.

He cautiously asked me questions in very halting English about her last movements. I had hoped to get her whole story but the state they were in made that impossible. They did say that they had promised her, if possible, that they would return with a doctor if they could find one and with some medical supplies. However, on the way down they lost their way and were only just able to find their way to Bagdora where I met up with them.

By then they were too consumed by guilt, sorrow and spreading panic. They believed that it was too late to find her again and it would be too difficult explaining what had happened besides they were too scared by then, scared of being detained, interrogated and in fear of losing their visas They had panicked. They had experienced something they scarcely understood.

Betrayal rarely ever is. I wonder if they had really escaped the mountain or whether it had them in thrall.

* * * * *

It was late in the sixth day when the bongthin reached Mt Kangchenjunga where the two rotmung had fled. Over the flint-sharp outcrop the shaman stopped. He called loudly into the wind. His voice carried far and wide into every crevice and pinnacle, and returned to him in dying eddies of sound. He sprang like a mountain goat from rock to rock as he crossed mountain streams, his white mane flying out behind him.

"Go back, go back!" called the rotmung from all around him. He heard their words above the cascades as freezing water swirled over between rocks.

A black cloud came rolling down from the rum-lyang, the land between earth and sky. The sun was blotted out and the sacred bongthin shivered. He wrapped his yak-hair cloak tighter around him. With a swift motion he managed to snatch back his staff from invisible preying hands. He leveled it in the direction of some mountain bramble in front of him. A loud crackling sprang out from the undergrowth. Some shrubbery was blown away up the sides of the mountain some down the side of the ravine. Cries of unendurable pain rang out in all directions.

"Find peace, shaman. Leave the mountain. You cannot have her. Such things come and go. That is as it has been and will endure. Go back!" shrill voices called from all sides and echoed on and on in the valleys.

The convergence of the mung, or evil spirits, made it difficult for the bongthin to advance any farther. He clung to his staff. As long as it was in his keeping the mung couldn't harm him.

"Go back, go back!" called the sharply insistent rotmung. The shaman's white beard and streaming white hair whipped about him, blurring his vision from time to time. There was a movement behind the clump of rocks. It was the mountain squirrel. At last his friends were catching up to him. He felt his strength returning. The wild boar couldn't be too far behind. The squirrel leapt on top of the largest rock, reared up on his hind legs and called out to him, "Oh shaman, look to tomorrow!. The fiery peacock arrives with certain death for the demons who fear it more than anyone else."

Up and down the ridges the trill of fear could be heard rising and falling in ripples as the evil spirits called to one another. Once or twice out there somewhere in the summit through mists, thunder rolled.

"You well know the way of life, shaman. You were there when the waters turned to rocks, when the winds were turned to flesh and bodies, and seeds were strewn in the valleys. Go back. Go back!"

The boar, the squirrel and the bongthin spent the lengthening hours together but as the hours passed, they knew the fiery peacock had withheld its support. The winds had died down. The whispering and whistling ceased as the mung folk made their way back over the conifers, rocks and ice to the eternal heights. Dark mists rolled up the mountain and the light from the sun broke through. They looked about them to see where they had landed.

Below in the valley the shaman saw the Long-thum monastery. Lamas were moving slowly about their morning devotions. The boar and the squirrel suddenly left him. He had turned to speak to them and to entreat them to stay with him, but he was now alone. He made his way down to the monastery. No one paid him any attention. He climbed the steps and entered the dim candle-lit interior. He met no one inside. When he came out again it was near the end of the day, but he no longer had his staff. Monks passed him by talking to one another as he strode past them up the steep goat track by which he had descended.

It took him a whole month to reach Kangchenzonga, but not before the rains set in. He was lashed by the sharp, cutting rain and high winds. In a clearing was the remains of the monkey temple. This was the land of the Rung-nyo-ung-dut who watched his every step. He stopped and looked at the ruins for a long time. He blinked mechanically from time to time. All emotions drained from his eyes. It would soon be night. Time to visit the village where the first fires for the evening meal would be burning. Then he heard her briefly, her voice drifting in the swirling winds.

"Shaman, lern vom Wind und vom Eis. Was ewig ist, wird night immer verstanden. Schauf auf die Spitze von Kangchengzonga und uberzeuge dich von dem, was unwandelbar ist und night vollends begriffen warden kann. Lausche dem Wind, bongthin. Was horst du?"

Ha! Learn the way of the wind and ice! He had his existence in their very midst. He should know that better than anyone. He was painfully aware of what could and could not be. The mountain had no power over him except when he gave it that power, if he ever did.

* * * * *

I felt the surge of creative fulfillment and a quiet exaltation. I stepped back from my canvas and cleaned my brushes. I used a knife to scrape off the extra hardened lumps of color I had allowed to form on my palette to be part of the picture. I washed my hands and dried them. It was all over. I have always wanted to live and move in the Himalayan mountains. I had often felt the surge within me. This was my first canvas after my return from Sikkim.

I looked at the painting again. I saw the mighty mountain, Kangchenzonga. I saw the shaman again. The demons. Ursula George. Rock and ice. The rotmung looked at me with a growing urgency.

I heard again the winds cry around the ruins of the temple. From the ageless peak came again the distant cry of the young woman. For just a moment it lived in the wailing of the winds. I lost the words, but none of the pain. Even though time and distance had restored to me the ability to separate my reality from the other, I knew in the other fall to come next year I would be preparing to fly out again, and into the mountains of Sikkim – to Kangchenzonga, where neither pain nor joy exist but the sheer mastery of the mighty mountain that rises up into the clouds, up above the transient flow of human life. It is there one stands on the threshold of two worlds.

LAMPSHADES
AND CUSHION COVERS

Eric Hausmann was brought to Australia by his grandson, Gustav, last year on a tourist passport. He had been diagnosed with a rare form of blood cancer. The doctors at Cologne Medical Centre were the best in the country in the treatment of blood cancer. They knew that an 85 year old cancer patient didn't have long. They advised him to enjoy what was left of his life. His granddaughter, Griselda, had been writing almost every week begging him to come to Australia on a farewell visit. The old millionaire had a very special spot in his heart for her. When she decided to settle in Australia and later married a doctor, Dr Peter Portelli, in Perth, it broke his heart. The doctor was a prominent oncologist and would be qualified to help the old man.

Old Hausmann decided he would go to her even if it meant his death. He persuaded Gustav to get him there. He was strong enough at present but would soon be incapacitated. It was a race against time. It was a race that Eric Hausmann won when he reached Australia at last. Gustav and Eric Hausmann were met at the airport by Griselda and her husband, Dr Portelli. With all the usual airport formalities behind them at last they sped away in Peter's BMW to Dalkeith where Griselda and he had their palatial home.

Old Hausmann settled in and seemed to enjoy being in Australia. He found the indigenous people a never-ending source of curiosity. He would like to have spoken to one or two but he was openly contemptuous of them just as he was of the number of Asian people he found in the shopping centres. That is why he began withdrawing from going to the shopping centres which he saw were institutionalized, that is, being a place for commerce as well as offering a social centre for people to mix and enjoy their days and evenings. This was offensive to him.

And so it was that when he was taken to the Rhine Danau Club in Melville he was overjoyed. Here was a place of refuge, a haven where only people of German extract were welcome it was claimed, although he discovered from time to time non-Germanic people, too, came and passed time occasionally. He resented it and queried the necessity of tolerating this from those he had come to know recently but found himself being patronized and even humored. He always hated that. He eventually cut himself off from most of them.

He also found himself isolated and ignored. At times he thought he caught some of them looking oddly at him but quickly averting their gaze when he stared them down. When he was picked up later in the evening by either his daughter or his son-in-law he tried to draw them into some discussion about his growing isolation but found they always changed the subject because they showed no interest.

Dr Hausmann would come into the Rhine Danau Club every morning at about 10am and order his first Heineken and take it to a darkened corner of the reading room, where a clutter of pot plants cut him off from the usual clients who had by then come to respect his desire for anonymity and seclusion. He browsed through some old German magazines scattered about on the tables. He sipped his beer whilst staring out at the world and ruminated on any item of news from Europe. Once in a while someone would come and take his empty glass and ask if he would like another, to which he usually nodded without looking up. The beer would arrive, he would mechanically pay and then retreat into the world of his own.

The Rhine Danau ran a number of interesting functions. There was the table tennis that could be played any time there were challenges afoot. Some preferred the endless rounds of darts that went on nearest to the bar. Every now and then cheers arose as some proof of great marksmanship became evident. At one far end there was a special corner for the TAB for those who liked a flutter. A race would be viewed in eager silence but soon there either followed a stream of profanities as the favorite was beaten or when a wager proved successful and then there would follow a call for drinks all round.

The Rhine Danau was "Ossified" German in culture. By which was meant that it was German without the politics although that would be passionately discussed by the oldest Germans who had come out of a war-ravaged Europe. Memories never dimmed but the patrons by and large managed to get rid of the vitriolic language of the Nazi dialectic. Where once hung photos of contemporary right wing die-hards now hung photographs of famous German soccer players.

For the literati there was a separate room that functioned as a Club library that held the German classics and contemporary philosophers and novelists. All the books were in excellent condition that might suggest they were not really patronized all that frequently thereby signifying the successful process of "Ossification" that was ineffably underway. And through all this sat the morose, lonely figure of the wealthy Hausmann. Time swirled past him in all its delusional ambience. The past never really deserted him. There were things he never ever let go, sadly enough.

On a stormy day in June one year the door of the Rhine Danau swung open to admit a tall over-coated figure of a silver-haired man. Despite his greying hair he exuded a boyish charm and inner health that could be referred to as a radiance. The Club manager, Roger Goltz, came out of his office and greeted him in a friendly manner as they shook hands. He invited the new-comer into his office with a shout over his shoulder to the barman, "Hans, two coffees, please. Make them strong and hot. That's the only way Dr Eleazar and I drink it. Right, Doctor? Come on in and tell me about your visit to Berlin. How do you like the new Germany?" Soon the voices died away as the door hissed closed. With this the two were soon ensconced in the luxuriously appointed office of the Manager of the Rhine Danau.

Closing time drifted into the Club which usually had very few left inside before that. The lonely figure by the palms remained unmoved. On this occasion a long shadow fell across his body. Nothing was said. The newcomer looked at the seated figure. The seated figure sat slumped waiting for his daughter. He looked at his watch once or twice.

"Hello, Herr Hausmann, I am Dr Eleazar. We haven't met. I have only this last week returned from Berlin," he said, to break the silence.

This was an intrusion that the old man hated. How dare the stranger imposed himself in this way. Where was the manager of the club? Why asn't he doing his duty more efficiently? The old man looked about the interior and snorted.

He made it obvious he detested the intrusion. The offer of politeness and friendship was ignored. It made for an awkward few moments. In the distance the anxious figure of the Manager could be seen hovering uncertainly.

Eleazar sat down without being asked to by Hausmann. He sat at the edge of the chair. Briefly he recounted his assessment of the new Germany and its multicultural composition. His voice echoed the cautious optimism of the new Germany that was unfolding.

"What do you miss most, sir, of the old Germany you knew and what you would like to revive?" asked Mr Eleazar.

The earlier silence returned but with a certain hostility. A fly buzzed past a plant and banged into the glass plate that cut off the outside world of the Club. A car was heard to pull up outside. Hausmann's daughter had arrived. The car door slammed and the clicking of her high heels could be heard.

"What did you say your name was?" asked Hausmann, without so much as looking up for a moment as the question was asked.

Almost eagerly the good doctor repeated his name, with a welcoming smile.

"Eleazar. David Eleazar. Dr Eleazar," he replied. "I was asking about what you missed most about the old Germany you knew, sir,"

The old man arose uncertainly on his feet and stared the intruder in the face. He advanced two feet up to the doctor and looked him up and down through two steely blue clouded eyes.

"Lampshades and cushion covers, Eleazar. You people made such damned fine lamp shades and cushion covers in Auschwitz and Belsen," he replied with a cackle. He drew himself up to his fullest, stared Eleazar in the face then brushed past him on his way out with a smile.

LIFE MATTERS DOT COM

The worst thing about Pretorius Zuma being unemployed for months was the low self-esteem that plunged him into a deadening sense of worthlessness. It had begun recently from the way his employer had dismissed him from service for reasons that were never made known. There was a suspicion that when questioned about the breaking of glasses in the lunch room he had on being questioned about it identified the culprits. If he hadn't he would have been fired anyway he was told by the manager.

It was the way they had gone about it and only because he was a black man. He had been humiliated by the giggling immature white teenagers who usually never got any work done but managed to keep their jobs. He had been led to the factory gate by a security guard who had held him by his wrist and virtually propelled him off the premises with a snarling, "Catch a bus up the road and don't come back."

He had stood with tears in his eyes looking back at the place of employment that had helped him to put bread on the table. Now what was he going to tell his wife. He wondered how his three children would take the news. He felt a sense of shame that became fear. He dreaded losing their respect.

From that day he regularly scanned the daily newspapers at the library. The Situation Vacant columns weren't any help. He had answered two advertisements but was disdainfully turned down. What were they wanting that he didn't have? He suspected it was his African black color that went against him. This was supposed to be a country that boasted racial equality. Only if you were white, he was convinced. He was beginning to wish he had learnt to live the Soweto life. Maybe he would have eventually succeeded in something. Maybe gang life would have offered him some sort of future. Selling crack would have been more rewarding, for sure. There was easy money to be made as a mule. He angrily dismissed the thought. He thought of the many friends whose lives had been shattered by the drugs the gangs sold. He had witnessed the treatment of those who fell into their debt and weren't able to pay the drug dealers. Tears filled his eyes. He thought of his younger brothers he had promised to bring to Australia when he had a steady job and a house or at least a flat. They had to be removed forever from harm's way. His widowed mother would be praying for him night and day. He felt shame at breaking her heart by his failures. He wanted her to know he was trying his best. He had to try harder. He urged her to keep praying for all of them. Prayer is the last resort of the weak and failing. Some attribute to it their successes and importance in their community. It wasn't your open sesame but you had to take your chance. Chance was one of the immutable laws in the universe.

He, Pretorious Zuma, had to try and get people, mainly would-be employers, wanting and prepared to give him his respect and a chance again. He had to succeed. To fail meant too many would die in poverty back home. He carried a great burden for them. It nearly robbed him of his confidence and self-respect. He felt himself sliding into a sickening depression. He knew he had to stay positive and remain strong. Too many were depending on him. He often thought of them, he often saw their faces staring at him. Their lips mouthed silent implorings and pleadings. It nearly sent him mad.

On one such day he had idly browsed through his emails The ancient XP was his only contact with the outside world and what kept utter despondency away. In an idle click of the cursor he read his favorite email from the well-known American theologian who ran a lecture site. It came up in a friendly response to his click. There it was. He smiled.

"Hello John Carver, sir. Nice to hear from you again. What do you have to say to me today?"

He peered into the monitor.

"Nil Desperandum

By John Carver

5/19/14

…...He resolved quietly "I will set myself the task of digging out past references on Buddhism and articles by the Australians I had heard about, good people like Louise Hay and Ian Gawler. I sought some balance from philosophical and spiritual equilibrium to help me cope with my recently diagnosed prostate cancer which…"

He was barely conscious of reading any further as he finished the article. John Carver was a good man whose sermons filled readers with hope and sense of worth. Surely the good God would take care of him and cure him. What ever you ask in my name that will I do, he had once taught. The end of the column supplied John Carver's email address and phone number in case anyone wanted to contact him.

Pretorius idly wondered how old John Carver was and if he had a wife and family. He wondered if he lived in a grand house like priests and bishops in South Africa lived in. With so many servants to look after their needs. What sort of car did he drive? One or two?

Many African middle class friends back home were better off, if not wealthier than Australians and yet many Australian families managed two cars. It would be nice if he could afford one.

May be one day...

Suddenly he found himself getting ready to hammer out a reply. He wondered if he would get into trouble. He wondered if he was being too presumptuous. But, he drew a big breath, squared his shoulders and decided he would communicate with Mr Carver.

He bent over his keyboard and thought deep and long, then began to peck out his message. He felt it brought him close to such a venerated Man of God. He felt humble and important in a role he was totally unqualified for, and well he knew that. But the message went out.

"Dear Master John Carver, I think I can cure your cancer. Please have faith in me. Buy three young and nearly ripened bitter gourds. Chop them into slices. Put them in a pan and cover them in water till they are just about immersed. Then bring the water to a boil. Turn off the gas and let the bitter gourd stand in hot water for half an hour. Drain the pan into a bowl and cool it. Then drink all of it and eat the fruit. It may taste bitter, but you must finish it. This must be repeated for at least a month. Longer if you prefer. Best wishes for good health, sir.

Pretorius Zuma"

He had no idea if the so-called Zuma prescription would prove successful since he hadn't tried it nor had anyone he knew tried it and survived. By communicating with such a good man he felt his equal and it restored his worthwhileness, even if momentarily.

Pretorius got on with life after that presumptuous moment at his computer.

One day as usual he was scrolling down his inbox when he found a reply from the famous John Carver. His heart pounded away in his rib cage. The reply was appended to his own email and it read: "So be it, Pretorius, I hope I will boil and drink forever!! You may yet be a famous man if this works!"

Pretorius smiled. Mr Carver sounded really friendly and even playful. He had found a famous friend. No one else in his real world was anywhere near as famous. He was going to tell everyone he knew and met all about the new company he enjoyed in his virtual world.

He printed the email that changed his world. Every time anyone derided him, laughed in his face Pretorius found strength in his himself to ride the bumps. He smiled in a tolerating manner his friends found strange and annoying. He wasn't fun any more. He had become unflappable. They looked at him strangely and began leaving off teasing him.

The day came when he even managed to get a job at a service station. He presented himself as a conscientious and polite man to management and customers. This was very pleasing to his employers who made him permanent. Pretorius worked harder than anyone else, almost with a crazy enthusiasm. He made the motorists feel as if they were valued customers. He chatted away as he cleaned the windows and wiped off smudges on the chassis. He would offer service that went beyond the usual and his customers were happy and had begun asking for him when ever they drew up for a refill the following week. They were grateful for such cheerful service and expressed their gratitude with tips. This made the other workers critical about his "crawling ways" to suck up to the boss and the stupid motorists who encouraged this behaviour.

The years passed happily enough for Pretorius and then one day he got an email from Mr John Carver. He read it happily. "Hi Miracle Man. You will be glad to know that I have been cleared of my prostate cancer! It appeared that the laboratory that carried out the testing for prostate cancer got the readings mixed up. I had been given the PSA of another person being investigated for the same cancer. When subsequent tests were run in another path lab my PSA showed up as normal. Another test was run and confirmed the good news. Thanks for your advice anyway. I still drink my bitter gourd elixir. It is now the subject of a sermon and a book I am currently working on. The title of the book will be 'Life Matters: Dot Com' May I use your name to make it authentic? Thanks again. Best wishes, John Carver." Ofcourse he could. What an honour. He was achieving a good name.

Pretorius felt mixed emotions. He was deflated somewhat because he had played no real part in Mr Carver's good health, but mainly happy and excited. He realized he had no basis on which to recommend any cures being largely uneducated and passing on as authentic mere hearsay. He would never tell anyone about it. He would never do such a thing again. The next time there may not be any happy conclusion. He might even kill someone. He shuddered at the possibility. No, he would never be so stupid again. He felt a new sense of responsibility where before he felt rejected and disillusionment with his life. Now he was a someone. Life was good. It had to be cared for and enjoyed in the right manner.

Of course John Carver must be allowed to mention his name. It may not be entirely to his, Pretorius Zuma's, benefit but at least he would go down in print. People would talk about him and his name would spread. How could he tell Mr Carver the truth? Fate throws you a life line and you should be grateful and use it to save yourself instead of throwing it back, he mused. He wondered if his mother and brothers would ever come to hear his story. When they get to Australia one day he would tell it to them. He had printed off the letter from Mr Carver and filed it away in a note book. He had saved it to his hard drive in case it got lost. It was valuable and needed to be carefully preserved. When you had nothing else in the world to recognise your place in it then it became imperative to look after what fate gave you as a substitute.

Others could benefit from the story. He trusted John Carver to use his name responsibly. John Carver was a good man. Those of you who now know about me must make up your own minds if I am a good person like they think of me at the Caltex service station.

Or just a shmuck trying to eke out a living in a harsh world.

LOBO

Lake Street car park is a motorist's haven on Northbridge. It spans the street into the heart of the disco world that comes alive only at night. It is the night that brings out the lovers and the predators. It is then that romance is most vulnerable but it evidently adds spice to the evening. Lasciviousness is set to primal rock music. What often happens then becomes headline news for the morning papers. That is how life goes on in the city where people try to hide out from whatever by dissolving into drugs, alcohol violence and sex hyped up by extra testosterone-laced romance.

The music of the night is the raw-boned hot rock or the love lorn chanting saxophone; it is the screeching of tyres and roar of the speed devils; it is the angry howling and flashing lights of red and blue of police cars and the wailing of police cars and an ambulance, it is the screams of abuse, the sounds of violent scuffles and cries of pain and cries for help and the sounds of running feet.

Half an hour ago I had received a call from my sister, Randa, to pick her up from the Night Life Bar and Bistro. She had been left by her date to find her own way back. That was just the trouble with women like her who demand to live their own lives against the advice of parents, brothers and other male members of families, and other well-wishers. I understood Randa's position of a young liberal Muslim woman who was highly educated and melding well into a non-Muslim world, and very successfully at that. Women like Randa want the best of two worlds but can only be sure of the pains of both. I understood it all too well as I was in much the same trap being very close to a beautiful German backpacker who I respected and came to love.

We really did not know Djamba, a highly westernized, qualified accountant and well-integrated Somali. He was born and bred in Australia and had played soccer for the Perth Glory some years ago. Randa had brought him over to the house a couple of times but on both occasions only for about half an hour. The meetings were little more than cups of tea and a round of cucumber sandwiches and suspended civilities. This was more out of a sense of duty and making peace with our parents. It was their way of testing the extent of our acceptance, our tolerance and the attitude of our parents. They were never happy with her choice of friend because they said that they had detected alcohol on his breath. I had not been able to support their accusations, not wishing to be a hypocrite, but eventually an unease set in between Randa and her family. There was something too "cool about the dude" let me say at the start so that I wasn't really surprised at the call. I sort of felt it was only a matter of time before this would happen.

So there I was headed to the Night Life Bar and Bistro. I thought that was where I should start my search. That was where they passed away their time most nights. When I got there it was very late and would soon be in the pre-dawn hours. I thought how ironic that their home away from home should be the "new life" in the bistro.

The New Life was still well patronized but those in there were all the worse for wear. The droopy-eyed bouncer was tired and filling up on copious cups of strong black coffee to help him keep just about half alert, and so didn't make any fuss and let me in. I searched the faces of the sleep-afflicted drinkers and those slumped at their tables too far gone to get up and go home and waited to be ejected. Randa was no where in sight. I asked the bald bar man if he knew where Randa was. I handed him a recently taken photograph of her. He took it and held it up to the light and nodded.

"You must be the one she talked about. If asked I was to give you this message," he said, handing me a note which read:

"Don t worry. Djamba and I have made up and I have gone with him. I am OK and so is he. Go home and tell them I shall be OK. Will get in touch one of these days? Now forget this change of mind. I am OK. Go home.

And also, I am sorry for the trouble and inconvenience. Love.

Randa"

I turned to ask the bald barman for more details about them but he had retreated to the farthest end of the bar to wipe and polish already shiny and clean tumblers and clearly indicated he had no wish to have any further communication on the subject. He looked at me with focused hostility and suspicion expecting trouble to erupt from me.

I spent the next hour walking up the streets in case I found them still together and hanging on to what remained of their patched up lives. This wasn't the first time for Randa. She was her own woman and had taken a flat where she hid from what she conceived as any cohesion at home with her parents and family members all of whom were very worried about her. The question we all asked each other was: How do we stop Randa? What should we have to do? We do not live in Afghanistan or Pakistan. We all lived in a new world. New answers were being sought but unsuccessfully.

The life she had chosen brought disgrace and dishonor upon us all. At the mosque we felt the cold shoulder of social ostracism, even if partly concealed behind reproachful smiles. Those who were our social detractors put on sly airs and graces, nothing overt but obvious for all that. Others with conservative agendas and recently from ultra-conservative backgrounds hissed their ignorant and spiteful answers as we came in and left. They were an ignorant and hateful lot, really.

Days passed turning into weeks and then into months. We were tempted to call in the police but we risked losing Randa forever. She would never have forgiven us, I warned our parents and other who were well-meaning and offered to do whatever they could to find her and get her home to us. Randa was a very stubborn woman who had every right to do what she was doing, establishing her rights in a country that allowed social contamination to run like a wild fire through families. We had come to accept that the police would not interfere if they located her and questioned her. We did not think she was entitled to do what ever she wanted with her life. Her life wasn't hers to live like this. This was what came with adopting blindly another culture most of which was acceptable but not all.

Then nearly a year later I was attending a business seminar at the Perth Business Centre in UWA when I saw the Somali sitting hunched over a sheaf of seminar papers. He was too absorbed to notice my approach. I was tempted to pull out my knife and cut his throat then and there but I managed to restrain myself. I waited and practiced a smile of sorts, with difficulty I might add. This was perhaps our last chance to find her. He felt my presence I think as he slowly looked up enquiringly to address the situation.

"Hello Djamba," I said but failed to hold out my hand with the greeting.

"Yes. I recognize you. What do you want? What can I do for you?" he said with ill-concealed truculence.

"Randa..." was all I could bring myself to say.

"Yes and what about Randa?" he asked spreading his hands to a sort of helpless inquiry. He cast a look of irritation at me.

"Please tell me where she is and how I can find her," I almost begged of the bastard. I hated myself for having to crawl to the black sod, even though I knew it wasn't all his fault, recognizing her part in the whole sordid business.

"If she wanted to go home she was always free to do so, let me assure you. As to where she is now I have no idea. To tell you the truth I don't care. She has caused me more trouble than I care to accept from her. We had been having our differences all along and were trying to sort out what we really wanted. Then one day I returned from University to find the place empty. All her belongings, few as they were, had been taken away. I looked about for her but was unsuccessful so I accepted the verdict. What else was I to do?"

Just then about four students, all from different ethnic backgrounds, were waving at us and calling out "Hobo! Lobo!" I didn't realise they were calling him till they were upon us and grinning. One of them put his arm around Djamba's shoulder. They looked at me wondering who I was and waiting for Djamber to introduce them to me which he didn't. This turned their attitude from being friendly to open belligerence.

"What you want, hey, man?" one of them, a pseudo-Jamaican sort I thought, asked me. To Djamba he then turned the question, "Lobo, then what he wan with you, my brudder?" The others mumbled similar questions. One of them turned to look me in the eye and pointedly drew a finger across his throat.

I knew it was wise to get away from what could turn out to be an ugly situation. Something sordid had begun brewing. I could feel it. I was outnumbered, and at a disadvantage. Djamba spoke to them in a foreign language and as I turned to go he called out, "I am not responsible for her, my friend. She does as she wants. Please let her loved ones know the truth about her. She is a lovely woman but..."

The others let out a leering mumble of what could only have been lascivious in nature and which I had no desire to find out. I left with a heavy and frightened heart as I realised that "Lobo" was a word from folkloric origins and meant "wolf". Was I drawing a long bow? The word had frightening connotations. Only for one last time I looked back at the group. He somehow didn't seem to be quite a natural part of them and was having to put up with some unwanted attention which he could well do without. He seemed as much a prisoner as Randa and I were as were the other the entire family members. I dreaded having to tell them what I knew. As I looked back I saw him still looking towards me, half smiling, as much for me as for them. This was how people like Djamba, Lobo, made their way through life, each a lone wolf and predacious. He surreptitiously waved weakly and very briefly at me. I stood looking back when they moved off. They called out some rather unsavory and unsolicited advice for me in between bouts of coarse laughter.

Randa had gone. No one wanted to believe she was dead but she might as well be. Only once did her name come up.

One day I met Djamba in Sydney where I was on a business visit. Things didn't go well for me as I tried handling a big deal that had gone sour and it was worse when I saw Djamba getting out of a taxi. Here was a new Australian who was gradually making it and realising his dreams but leaving a trail of victims in his wake and not caring very much about it. He wouldn't care who he hurt on his way to what he conceived as the top. He was totally self-centred. Today here he was, rather smartly dressed. Our eyes locked briefly. After the briefest of pauses he shook his head slowly signifying he had nothing new to hand over to me. Then he was gone. I didn't see any point in telling an aging and ailing mother about the meeting. It would only add to her grief. Living in a new and dominant culture families found that sacrifices were going to be made, like it or not. This could breed violence or it could lead to a troubled assimilation, especially in multi-cultural societies. Australia wasn't always going to blame, Lobo was a Somali who had come from half way around the world with all his hates, his personal ambitions, heartbreaks and aggressions and demands.

MUJA MUJA

Muja Muja was a property lost in time. No one can recall to this day how the property got its name which was supposed to mean, "Dark. Dark." Indigenous people keep well away. It was well over a hundred years old but no one would have seriously considered awarding it a heritage listing.

There was the sprawling bungalow around which ran a verandah that was partly bounded by a winding and uncovered road that drovers might have made good use of many years ago. It seemed ancient but it also promised a sense of not so distant history. Along side it was something like a granny flat, what could have been a two-bedroom house, of more recent vintage. It had some thin semblance of a kitchen garden though no evidence existed of any active cultivation having been done in months. It stood close to what appeared to be a sealed road. On either side of the road grew weeds almost waist high, green in winter months but a withered brown in summer, when it became derelict with age and mortality.

It appeared on a regional map as a dotted line and flattered with the name of Covich Road. Occasionally a car would drive past stirring up a trail of dust. It must be admitted only kids high on testosterone sometimes, especially at week ends, came to race madly about, roaring defiance to a world that was out of sympathy with their existence, or being chased by a police car in hot pursuit.

They loved taking on the cops whom they baited even if later on it landed them in a cell, after which their parents would be contacted to appear and pick them up. All this was considered fun and better than anything on TV or at the motorplex.

Muja Muja came to be owned by the Saradov family who had emigrated from Croatia some years ago. The land and property then had been going cheap and friends and relatives advised them to buy it. Exactly how they found the finance and how exactly the deal was made was never known but there were rumours that floated around. That was how it came about that Marija and Tony Saradov came to be the present occupants.

Marija Saradov was alone one day. She liked everyone to call her "Marija" sounding the "j", and not "Maria" as it should be pronounced. No one knew why she wanted this. There was a lot about Marija and her eccentric husband, Antonio, that most neighbours knew very little. Not even that they were sixty odd years of age although they looked parched and unkempt enough to appear octogenarians. The Saradovs cherished a sort of anonymity. Some sort of disability had won them a pension which had enabled them and their two offsprings to live on. The boy was the elder and was said to be in and out of gaol and the girl kept having babies somewhere in Western Sydney.

About ten years ago Marija and Antonio's cousins had joined them from Croatia and built a small house on the property. They were seldom seen there. They were a secretive lot and pretty much kept to themselves. There were times they left the place. No one knew where they went for long periods of time. They came and went mysteriously. It was doubted that even the Saradovs quite knew where this was. No one bothered asking. What went on in and around Muja Muja was no one's business but theirs alone. It was a lot safer that way. But just the same an unwarranted suspicion about illegal activities nourished the idea based on their furtive habits and unkempt appearances. This perhaps might have been grossly unfair, but the Saradovs would have been partly to blame for all this. They lived unfriendly lives, living apart from the rest of the world.

One summer day at about midday Marija was sitting out on the verandah wicker cane chair when she saw a cloud of dust rising. It followed an old Ford ute that was flying like a bat out of hell. Here was an instance of a cliché that was the most appropriate way of putting it. Crazy racing was a familiar enough sight so that Marija paid no real attention to it. It would soon be gone, as it bounced from rut to rut. She and her husband had grown accustomed to all this. They were usually young hoons hell bent on living like lunatics. This one was no different. They were all hell bent driving all over the place. Not this one, she thought. It had come and gone many times before.

But it would be going nowhere this last time.

On this occasion something made her turn to look and when she bothered to have a look she saw the Ford ute become airborne. The pathetic ute seemed to get suspended for a few seconds after which it executed a graceful flip over. It landed with a loud thump and rolled twice and came to a halt on its cabin. The wheels spun crazily in the red cloud of dust. Nearby magpies rose as one, cawing desperately and fearfully, as they flew away from the wreck. When the red dust cloud it had kicked up settled Marija shook her head.

The idiot had it coming. She rose and went inside when minutes later she saw the flashing of red and blue lights of a police car that had chased the fugitive, siren wailing like a banshee, all the way along Covich Road. Once at the scene the police car came to a halt. Two police officers jumped out and slammed the pursuit car's doors as they ran to the ute whose wheels were spinning crazily.

This was getting quite exciting, she thought with a great deal of relish. Marija went to the refrigerator and calmly took out a can of Fosters and opened it with a well-practised flick of the metal tag. She swigged a deep mouthful of the bubbling fluid and belched contentedly. This was police drama of the very best kind. All real, and not on the tube like all the other car chases that no longer excited her. She let out a short laugh and took another swig and sat down. Antonio would be sorry he missed out. He had left her again for too long. Serve him right. He lived for crashes at the motorplex outside Kwinana. She took her can of beer and went casually out on to the verandah and resumed her sitting on her favourite chair. This was the life. She sighed contentedly. There was a time, quite recently, as a matter of fact, when they had it really tough and they felt that life had been so unfair but things were getting better.

The two officers, a man and a woman, had run to the wreck and were desperately yanking at the door to extricate the driver. From where she sat she could hear the agonized screams of the youth. The male officer then walked a couple of steps about the wreck calling on his phone. It must have been for an ambulance and tow truck to get there as soon as possible. Covich Road being no where in particular, these calls would be answered in due time but not soon enough to save the driver, as was later revealed. By now most of the dust devils had left the scene of the carnage and the spinning wheels could be seen coming to a halt slowly. The policewoman worked all the while relentlessly applying CPR but realized eventually it was to no avail. She arose and brushed her hair back from where it had come away in her exertions.

Then the two officers turned and looked up to where Marija was sitting. They conferred briefly. The female officer stayed with the body of the driver which was half out of the vehicle whilst the man began making his way up to Marija. His steps were laboured as he toiled up the slope to where she sat. He fumed at the indifferent spectator who was smiling and holding out the can of beer as if she was offering him a drink.

All he said under his breath was one word: "Bitch!".

They spoke for a few minutes, the woman proving an obstruction to his preliminary investigation. He warned her it was an offense obstructing the course of an investigation for which he could take her in for further questioning with a possible arrest if her attitude persisted. He felt his patience rapidly running out. He couldn't understand her attitude. Nevertheless, he patiently as he could, continued questioning her, looking across to where his partner remained with the body of the young driver. She looked up now and then and wondered what was keeping him. It wasn't a serious problem but an open and shut case.

"And how far do you think that will get you?" she said with a sneer." I didn't see a thing, as I have told you over and over again. I was inside when I heard the crash. When I came out I saw the wreck. I don't have a phone so I couldn't phone any cops or the hospital. And no, I don't have a mobile, either. I have been suffering with episodes of unstable angina so I wasn't going to walk down to see if I could be of any help. I hate these hoons and I wouldn't lift a finger to save a hoon's life, but that isn't a crime. If it was, half the community would be behind bars, but then there wouldn't be enough cells to accommodate the lot of them. I suspect you too would qualify for jail time, too, wouldn't you? Go on, tell the truth, now."

She then finished her cigarette and stubbed it out and moved past the big body of the policeman and looked out to where the wreck was. She looked passively on, a slow smile splayed across her face. She smiled with a curl of her lips and a lack of mirth in her eyes that were narrow slits from which ran many furrows of her disposition. Clearly there had to be good reasons why she had such an issue with police enforcement officers.

"Take a look at where your partner is. It's all over. Go away. You have been wasting your time. She needs your help. You won't get anything from me, officer. So piss off, now." she said.

When the burly policeman turned to look at the wreck and his partner he saw the tow truck come bouncing down as it hit rut after rut. Behind it came an ambulance as it, too, rocked from side to side. Clouds of dust flew from both of them obscuring each partially. At the scene of the accident the tired and sweating policewoman had got to her feet and stood looking up towards the house, a wind playing with her hair. She waved her hand slowly signifying the driver had died in the wreck. She looked up into the sky. No matter how often one attended such a scene one never really got used to the waste of life that had returned to inert matter.

The ambulance arrived shortly after the tow-truck. The male policeman had come down at long last having failed to secure any co-operation from the woman. There was nothing more he could have done. The paramedics felt the same way. After a short discussion they too saw that there was nothing to be done except to cover the corpse, take it into the ambulance and pull the wreck on to its wheels. There wasn't anything there they could discuss so they presently clambered into their vehicles and pulled away. The policeman looked out from the driver's side window, slowed right down to take another look at Marija and gave her a nonchalant wave. He said something to his partner who showed no sign of having heard as she looked the other way. He gave a guttural laugh and spat out of the window. With an oath, he made the police car lurch forward aggressively as they left the scene of the fatality.

THE STRENGTH OF WEAKNESS

Through out history human beings have looked at the changing faces of weather to placate it, to thank it for blessings and to worship it in its many manifestations only to be rewarded it by an implacable indifference.

The depression wasn't passing over as promised by the Weather Bureau. It was proving stubborn and unrelenting, bringing sharply dropping temperatures and non-stop showers, many very heavy at times. Light poles had come crashing down in some suburbs. Hundreds of homes had been without power for the past forty-eight hours. Repair crews had worked as fast as they could but even as power was restored in some areas when another suburb was plunged into darkness. It wasn't so much that people were without power to cook their meals but many more lived in very cold homes. Many were aged and infirm, and many were sick and bedridden. Hospitals and shelters were unable to cope. Paramedics and volunteer drivers were struggling to answer desperate calls for help. What made matters more critical were the growing number of accidents on the roads. Tow truck operators were being kept busy at all hours.

Clovelly Crescent was within a stone's throw of the central business district in Carlisle. It was where the very comfortably-off lived. It was well-served by security patrols during the night and that was probably what kept the residents safe in their beds. Only very rarely did one hear of someone's house being broken into. On this night in particular the thin mist and steady rain had transformed street lights into mere dim orbs with ghostly halos that didn't light up the streets. The picture was at best an extension of the inner life of most people here in Clovelly Crescent, dim and frosty and filled with fear and uncertainty and not suited for much communication. It wasn't the best of times; in fact, it was about the worst of times.

Dinner over, Jeremiah Dearborn Sr prepared to settle down with a copy of the day's "The Age" newspaper and study the stock market fluctuations of the day. Recently it had been making rather unhappy reading. He sipped his Single Malt Bushmill whiskey appreciatively. It was more than merely a luxury that he preferred to his many others. It restored his peace of mind and helped him to sleep easily. The lights dimmed for a moment and he cursed quietly to himself. Light had only been restored about an hour ago. He went over to his cabinet drawer and took out a battery-operated emergency light should the lights fail again. He planned to get to bed early and get a good night's rest. Maybe tomorrow would bring better weather.

On his way upstairs to his bedroom he cowered as lightning flashed threateningly and there followed a loud crashing of thunder that reverberated for a few seconds. It was going to be a bad one. Through the window he saw a branch of a tree flash past, borne along by the force of a powerful gust that had torn it from a near by gum tree. He felt the tremors as the wind crashed into his Clovelly Crescent mansion. Every flash of forked lightning revealed something a little of the power of nature. Lightning always revealed the vulnerability of human beings. That night he had also seen something else.

An elderly man with six children all huddled together stood outside, all soaking wet. One who was partly concealed must have been the mother. Dearborn Sr was momentarily undecided. She was clearly traumatized as must have been the children. Why were they out in this weather and why were they without a home in which to be secure? Dearborn Sr was a sort of man to whom such facile observations came readily.

Here was a dilemma to be solved. He paused, but not for long, as he decided it was not his problem though the children were wet, hungry and clearly terrified as the tempest roared about their ears and the lightning flashes seemed to be getting nearer. At the head of the landing he stopped and turned back. He would like to have gone to bed but there was a conscience that weakly stirred for a while at the moment and left him undecided.

The man began knocking on the door. He probably wouldn't stop till something was done for him and his family. Dearborn Sr was more than a little annoyed that they had made their problem his. They had the rest of the world to whom they could have made their nocturnal appeal. The children had given the problem a moral edge. This was how every catastrophe in the world acquired its moral edge. Dearborn Sr felt that the parents knew all about that. They played the family as their trump card. It worked a treat for many others. He readily recalled the warning from the great Bard himself, "Sweet are the uses of adversity." It was happening all over again here in Clovelly Crescent, Australia. He slowly descended the stairs and opened the front door. The children pushed to gain entrance to the dry and warm interior. Fear shone from their staring eyes. One of them whimpered when thunder rolled across the night sky. It was fortunate for all of them that the winds had dropped and the rain was a mere drizzle. Dearborn Sr closed the door behind him and prevented them having access to his home. Whatever was going to transpire would begin from there, outside the mansion. He pulled his coat closer about him. He hated them for inconveniencing him in this way. Something had to be done immediately. He could send them off on their way to knock upon another door or he could help in some way more for the sake of the children. He loved his many grandchildren and well he understood their vulnerability.

"Please, dear sir, we beg refuge from the storm and for some food and water. We are starving," begged the man. What must have been the mother of the children gave support with an odd high-pitched whine Dearborn Sr could not understand. They said nothing yet to say why they were in such a vulnerable position. Why had that been left unsaid? Where had they been living before this? He could not understand what had led to this crisis. Perhaps what he should do was to tell them about institutions like The Salvation Army and how to approach other such institutions that regularly took in people under such circumstances.

Shaking his head disapprovingly as if he were acting reluctantly Dearborn Sr had brought out a set of keys and a torch which he held in his hands. It was now switched on. He suggested that they go to the shed at the rear. It was big and well lit. They would be more comfortable there and better protected. Some food would be brought for their needs once they were settled down. It was the best that he could do for them. The man protested humbly pointing to the many bedrooms such a big, roomy house must have. There would be room enough and even more than enough for everyone. The wife would need a special and more suitable room for herself and the children.

In the shed Dearborn Sr opened a cupboard and showed them where there were blankets and pillows for everyone. They would be warm and would sleep well. There was water and tin provisions in the cupboards. There were biscuits and cheese in plenty. In the morning when the storm had abated and the rain had eased they could go on their way back from where they had come. Dearborn Sr wouldn't be asking what had brought them to this state and what they intended to do about it. Somethings were best left unknown. Dealing with the present was enough. He vividly recalled the ancient Chinese proverb, "Save a man's life and you are responsible for him for the rest of his life"...or something like that. The man volunteered the information himself. He formed his own question and thought that was the best way of telling the man some of their pathetic story. It really wasn't considered very convincing, anyway.

"From where we have come? But that house has come down in the storm, sir. There is no home left. We would like to stay here. We love this place. We have often walked past your house, sir. We admire it. God has been kind to you. You have been blessed. My wife says she will be very safe and comfortable and so will our sons, sir," said the man.

God kind to him?

Huh, he snorted under his breath. The fool clearly was trying to flatter him or trying to lay upon him a sense of communal obligation. He didn't know anything of his divorce and the previous death of his son. But he decided to attack the present and deal with the problem confronting him.

"At the height of the storm you and your family walked kilometers to reach my house but you did not think of asking the other householders to take you in. You were not concerned for your health and safety but came here instead. Now you insist on me giving you refuge here," replied Dearborn Sr, getting more suspicious and more than a bit angry. "Why didn't you try asking others to take you in and give you shelter and food for the children and your wife? You are their protector and provider. You should be doing better than coming here to me. You should be ashamed of yourself. Where is your sense of responsibility to your children and to your wife?

You aren't entitled to pick and chose whose house and hospitality you can demand. No. I will not oblige you and your people. In the morning I expect to find you gone. Take only as much bread and cheese you need. I will need to clean up after you." He returned to the interior of his home and turned a deaf ear to the pleading intercessions of the man and his wife.

Closing the front door, presently Dearborn Sr finished his fill of whiskey and a cheroot and then he changed into his night clothes and went to bed. He couldn't have been too upset. He soon fell asleep. Sometime before dawn he heard the sound of something banging. He rubbed the sleep from his eyes and sat up suddenly.

The door of the outside extension which he had made available to his nocturnal visitors was open and swinging open and shut making the hellish din. Why hadn't they secured the door? Then it came to him in a flash. They must have left the place. He pulled his dressing gown about him and slipped into his shoes and went down stairs. Looking out he could see that they had gone and left the door open to the weather. He took his torch and went out to investigate. The storm had abated somewhat but still vigorous enough to make him force his way through its gusts. This was a storm of quite another dimension. He felt that he may not have dealt with it in the most approved manner. His actions may well be criticized once it came to be known what had transpired. He didn't feel guilty; not really. He had done the best he could. He hadn't merely turned them away.

He found that nothing had been taken. The bed had not been slept in, nothing seemed to be missing. Here was the moral imperative again. Or was it a moral imperative? The man had further exposed his dependents to the terrible night out of a sense of pride. There was a good chance that they could now possibly fall ill. He had rejected the humiliation, which would have been the way he chose to interpret what had happened to him and to his loved ones. It made Dearborn Sr quite angry. He had no right to do that. He couldn't just think of himself, for himself. He should have been strong enough to sacrifice all that for the sake of his family.

He had just successfully stood strong against an attempted exploitation by the weak against the strong. The principle was slowly and covertly creeping into the emerging history of the world these days.

SEND FOR ELIAB

Overhead vultures explored the air currents that were cooler than the burning earth below. When they looked down on the brown earth they would have seen very little life. The earth was a hostile and rocky place of little promise, that had once been cursed by an evil god. Vultures rarely descended in a search for life.

In the middle of what once looked to be a pasture, stood a broken down red tractor. It stood stranded in scorched tall grass and weeds. It listed to one side. This was the scene that the traveller examined from afar as he wiped the perspiration from his brow. He stood gazing in the pain of recognition. Nothing much had changed despite the neglect and desecration of time. He recognized it, nevertheless, though he had been gone these last twenty or so years. In all that time no word had reached him about the history of those years. As a much younger man, he had ridden on the tractor as he went about his work during harvest time. He remembered the times it had broken down and he and Dathan had scavenged parts and repaired the tractor. It couldn't go on like that. He had begged the old man many times to get a new tractor but his pleas fell on deaf ears. They could have afforded it, but Dathan wouldn't support his demands. Dathan was the elder son and the favorite.

Eventually Eliab lost interest in farming. The hardened earth had hardened the core of human life. He shook the earth off his hands. He undertook other duties but was always asked to do something else he didn't care for. Whatever he did wasn't good enough. Dathan rarely spoke two words to him before the sunset on any one day. His father coughed and spat and brushed past him when he happened to be in his way. There was usually a muttered curse about something. Painful memories came flooding back. This was his old homeland. The earth, the trees and the rocks made him feel he was home. It was a curse from hell that had brought him into this family.

Eliab spat into the dust bowl from the side of his mouth. He descended the slight declivity and rounded the shoulder of a slight outcrop of rock that held pockets of earth, home to scrawny weeds and a basking lizard that scuttled away as Eliab came round the shoulder. His feet shifted slightly in some loose earth and rubble ran away from under his feet that fought for balance.

Before him stood the old family home, now a tired-looking mass of timber and a corrugated iron roof. A wind blew through the broken window panes. The front door was ajar. I seemed that it might have been accidentally left open, or deliberately, as if it was certain that there was no further use for the house. There was no coming back: nothing to come back to. It was sad to reflect on the life to which it now stood witness. Ghostly echoes of children's laughter in play seemed to linger. Every now and then a woman's voice was to be heard calling, calling, followed by excited shouts from children at play. He thought he recognized his own voice calling for mother. The dancing afternoon dust devils carried the voices away in successive phantom cries.

An emaciated dog sadly stared vacuously through eyes that lacked light in them, and were merely lusterless orbs. It lifted itself with a great effort and slunk away with a limp into the interior to escape, if it could, the flies that now even tormented Eliab. Its rib cage protruded miserably, poor thing. He wondered where it came from and whose it was. They had never had a dog that he could remember.

The wind flapped his damp shirt around his perspiration-saturated back. He turned when again he seemed to hear that woman's voice again. It was the voice of his mother. He still couldn't decipher what she was calling out. The words swirled too quickly into the darkened interior. He loved his mother the most and leaving her was not easy. She haunted his thoughts into depression till time ate away the hard edge of the sadness and left only a very persistent sense of guilt and depression that he could not shrug away.

Eliab cautiously entered the house. Curtains hung like ghosts in tatters and danced around in macabre fashion every time the wind blew through the empty house. The sofa was still there, the stuffing half out. Everything was coated with thick dust that flew up as he passed his hands over them. Nearby stood two upholstered chairs that also had all the signs of tragic abandonment, now home to dust and spiders. He walked around the lounge, each foot-fall sounding muted on the dust-laden carpet. He approached the escritoire which stood against the wall. The faded Degas print looked sadly back from above it. There had been happier times, it seemed to say. He stood looking at the table-top wistfully. This is where the old man conducted his business and determined the family fortunes. Eliab wondered what had led to this show of destitution, what calamity that spread before him. The enormous emptiness of his old home brought a sob from his parched throat. Unsuccessfully he searched for a secret history. He searched for a clue to the tragedy. Life had disintegrated rapidly, it seemed. Why?

Again the anguished cry as tumbleweed came dancing in when another gust swept past him. Through a broken window he saw it as it came to a halt in the distant corner to join a collection of former detritus. This time it carried the bass mutter of the old man's dissatisfaction about some domestic detail. He heard girls cry out demanding something or another as the girls were wont to. Eliab smiled sadly. Many memories struggled to register in his feverish mind.

He wondered where Miriam had gone. She would be married by now. There would be children. He wondered who her husband was and how they could have met and where they might have met. There was no trace of her. He had got on well with her especially the day after he found her out in the bush somewhere she had fallen from her horse and hurt her ankle. He had carried her home. She became very close to him and supported him against the wiles and bullying behaviour of Dathan. He had tried to keep his brother out of his thoughts all this time. He was one reason he had to leave home and seek his own fortune far away in the big cities. There was no love lost between them. Nothing ever went right for the brothers. One reason was because the father loved Dathan more and didn't mind showing it. For Dathan there were only smiles; for him,

Eliab, there were only scowls and a show of annoyance. And his mother pretended she never noticed all this. When he had complained she shook her head and told him to run away and play and not to imagine things like that. It filled his heart with sorrow and anger.

In the end all this proved beneficial because one day he left and went far away to make a life for himself where he believed he could be happy. He didn't have to wait too long. Things looked up for him. Things did go his way. He soon got work digging ditches at first and then he worked in fields for farmers. There was no shortage of menial work. Having no special skills, he knew no other way of working. In time to come after living frugally he had saved a small fortune and bought a small farming property and had built a solid future as a farmer in a distant valley where he met and married the orphaned Sarah. They had no offspring as yet. He doubted that they ever could. He suspected their time might have already past to have children. The thought was always accompanied with a pang of sorrow for both of them.

His past never left him. Days and months would pass without it stirring in his deep consciousness and he would shrug it off. Then he would hear his mother. Then he would hear his sisters laughing. Then he felt he would like to get a glimpse of home because home it still sadly was. It held him in thrall. It was like the stirrings of a guilty thing. The devil's grasping hands tore at his mind. When the news came it came unbidden. He had met a stranger at an inn. They had had a few drinks and got talking and eventually Eliab realized the story he was getting was really about the property that lay like a ghost without any tenants or owners. The description was a clear enough indication. On through sly questionings Eliab learnt of its fate, of what had befallen the family. Some details of the stranger's story were garbled and weird but that was the way of all gossip.

All this passed through his mind as he wandered about the echoing house where invading currents of air stirred sounds from distant times. At times he had to stop and listen and try to catch the words. The library was full of cobwebs. This was an area of the house he very rarely visited. There had never been a reason to. Books meant nothing to him. His father never shared it with any one.

His hand reached down to the right hand drawer. It mildly protested with a whine, being disturbed after all these many years. He rummaged about. None of the accumulated papers meant anything now. There was a manila envelope that caught his interest for some idle reason. So he opened it and withdrew a folded sheet of paper. He felt he was intruding and that he shouldn't be doing this. He sat down in a puff of dust and began reading.

As he read, a picture slowly came to mind. It was a letter to his brother who, after all these past years, had come to live an estranged life from the family for some unknown reason. There was no evidence about any sort of rift or enmity that had come to separate them. It was all so strange. When he looked more closely at the letter, he saw it had in fact been a letter that Dathan had returned to his father, without comment. It wasn't a very lengthy letter, but what hammered Eliab's heart was what must have been the last request of his aging father to his favourite son, a request that had been earnestly been made to Dathan, a request, couched in urgent tones. The only words that burned into Eliab's mind were "Send for Eliab." That was all. "Send for Eliab".

The words jabbed him with a sadness that he had never experienced before. Now that it had hit him, it hit him forcefully. He gasped and sat down. Dathan could not bring himself to reply to the impassioned request for assistance. His father had admitted to needing him. His father.

It was a dying man's last request that the favourite son had felt unobliged to fulfil. He crumpled the paper in his fist and withdrew a box of matches and burnt it and watched it crinkle into black carbon waste which curled up, now red-rimmed as the flame died out. He wanted to hate that brother but a stronger emotion washed over him. His heart broke as he recalled getting word from a stranger who had spent days looking for him to carry the news of the death of his parents, first his father and soon after his mother who refused to live a day as a widow.

He wondered why he had bothered to return to the empty house when there was nothing to be done. There was no one to meet and no one to greet him. He wondered if Sarah had heard the news and if she had come secretly and buried his parents but was too frightened to tell him, hoping that he wouldn't find out. There was a chance that he wouldn't. A new flood of a strange emotion filled his heart as he thought of Sarah. He recognized the feeling as love.

He looked around the house slowly and hoped they hadn't died alone. Dying should always be a farewell of love. He heard a noise and looked up. The lean and starving dog stood at the door, its head drooping. Only half of the dog was to be seen. It was too afraid to come any further.

SHAFA

Many African countries border the great Sahara Desert, the cruelest expanse of burning, inhospitable and lethal stretch of sand in the world. Through its history it has determined the fate of many travellers, traders and armies most of whom have left their bodies swallowed in the desert sands and whose names are no longer remembered.

Now, in the twenty-first century, after many millennia, it still offers traders avenues to cross many countries as itinerant traders plied a precarious trade in spices, clothes and even drugs and prostitutes. In the present century new hundreds of thousands have increased their numbers are on the move with with new cargo, carrying terror and pain and suffering, some desperately looking for freedom and a better way of life to escape the life in the hovels and camps and terror. And the graves in the desert waste lands are growing at a tragic rate all over again. The lure of happier and a more fruitful life are built up by tales filtering through to sub-Saharan, Saharan and forest lands bordering the great sandy waste lands that a better and happier life in Europe calls out to them and their families who are desperate and brave enough to take the risks.

They had no idea where to go or to whom they could turn for help. One such refugee trying to escape with her family of five was a fourteen year old girl who, because of the starvation she grew up in, was undernourished and stunted in growth. She lived in and was nurtured in a family that grew up in a small rural town of Kantsche in Niger. Her father had died about five years ago. Relatives had demanded of her mother to marry her off to rich uncles or old and sometimes almost toothless powerful elders from other neighbouring tribes.

Her adventurous mother, Rashas, had decided to join up with some others to face a dreadful death and make the fateful journey to a better future. They had been told stories about a huge expanse of water in the north that separated the desert from a fertile land overflowing with milk and honey. They sold every cow and goat they owned to raise the money they said would be enough to buy their safe arrival in this mythical land. If they failed they would be plunged into a lifetime of prostitution and poverty. It would make slaves of all of them.

They told each other that if they stayed together they would be strong and no one would be able to harm or stop them. It was faith in this belief that gave them strength to undertake this madness. There were altogether ninety two of them on this journey for a better life. They didn't have to look hard all over the world to find agents to make the necessary arrangements; the agents found them out to talk them into their protection. Those who needed this "protection" unhappily were desperate, ignorant and the willing who easily later became victims of cruelty and depravity.

They were impressed by the confident demeanour of their protectors and men who promised to be their saviours. What impressed them all the more were the two trucks that they owned. They took it in turns to ride in the two decrepit Ford trucks that had been stolen by two Malian soldiers who were deserters from the army and worked as protectors making a fortune out of the misery of poor people. They took nearly all the money these unfortunates had.

They were evil-looking and had very black skin from which yellow reptilian eyes darted rapidly right and left menacingly. One of them kept an eye on Shafa who felt it wanted to devour her so she clung to her mother in fear. These two soldiers of fortune only had two machetes with which to fight off slave traders and also to maintain order and obedience to them.

Two days into their odyssey of hope they struck disaster. In the afternoon one of the trucks lurched and broke down beyond repairs in the middle of the Sahara Desert. This could only mean one thing - with only one truck left many would now have to be left to die, or many would have to trudge across the burning dunes or live cramped inside the remaining truck. The Malians tried herding as many as they could into the one remaining truck. These were the aged, infirm and women and children. The men, young and old alike, would have to walk along side the best way they could. Stragglers, the infirm and old would be left behind to die. During one of the comfort stops Shafa's older brother, Hanu, and two of his friends ran about playing among the dunes despite being repeatedly called back. Each time they said that they had to answer the call of nature before the journey re-started. Being children they laughed, chased each other about the dunes and took their time to answer nature.

Suddenly all eyes turned to the ridge from where they heard the sound of a car approaching. Through the shimmering heat waves they could make out a jeep. The Malians unsheathed their machetes. Above the sound of the car they heard the screams of the three boys. Men and women ran to see what had happened to them. Shafa was slow in keeping up. She saw them scatter wildly as a jeep bore down upon them with no attempt to avoid running any of them down. Their deadly intentions were manifestly clear. The three boys clawed their way to the top of a dune screaming to their parents to save them. From the jeep a withering outburst of AK 47's roared out and the three rolled over, blood pouring from their wounds. For a while one or two bodies twitched about before they became lost in death. They never saw Hanu again. He must have fallen at the bottom of the declivity. The bodies of the other two who had been his playmates lay fallen on the surface where they twitched their last in their blood.

Six soldiers in battle fatigues descended, weapons held firmly before them. They wore raybans that gave them a fiendish appearance. They singled out the Malians and swore at them as they called them to come up to them and kneel down. The Malians began a loud weeping and begging. They knew what was going to happen to them. They were kicked about and beaten savagely and asked to hand over the fares which the Malians were only too happy to surrender.

The leader of the five mercenaries, a figure of some authority, lighter in his complexion, more Mediterranean than African, counted the loot and shared the proceedings to the satisfaction of all. At an order the five others trotted to the truck and made a quick search of its interior but found nothing they wanted. They shouted the information to their leader whilst he walked up to the kneeling Malians and unholstered his Glock and casually fired into the back of their heads almost at point blank range. The Malians rolled over quite dead, their brains and blood spurting and then running into the sand which absorbed it close to their bodies. The execution sent the African refugees into frenzied and panicked wailing. Rashas clung tightly to her Shafa covering as much of her as she could in her shawl.

Whatever the jerrycans still contained of their meagre supply of water came pouring out into the hot dunes when the raiders fired into them. After the jeep disappeared over the sandy ridge the men and women broke up into separate groups each with their own guess which route to take to death. Rashas took Shafa with her to a group they had known and some they had befriended. No one really had any idea where they were and much less where to go, but it was important to die together. But Shafa didn't die. A UN Medecin San Frontiere's plane found her hours from death, wandering around in a blinded daze, vultures circling around her emaciated body. It was fate that ordained that she alone should survive her ordeal. Whatever happened to the others has never been formally acknowledged but there has been no record of any other survivors. Shafa's story was never taken seriously and followed up. There were just too many similar stories nearly every week to follow through, and little or no resources on the ground to help.

A Medecins San Frontiere aircraft landed and took her to an emergency base, before transferring her to a town better equipped to restore her in body and mind. Later, after Shafa had completely recovered in a Strasbourg hospital, she was able to slowly and uncertainly offer her UN carers and doctors an account of sorts of the entire episode. The UN agency for refugees organized a search party to scour the desert to look for any other survivors. They didn't find any, but along different trails leading off in different directions they managed to find partially uncovered skeletons. When they dug around the remains they uncovered the awful, inhuman tragedy. It became apparent that here was a small paragraph to be written into the bloody criminal annals of crimes against humanity.

Shafa grew up in her twenties working as a young, beautiful nurse for the international organization that had saved her life. A Turkish doctor became her constant companion. She trusted him even though he had made it clear that there wouldn't be any future in it for them. One day he would have to return to Izmir where his family lived. He was aware who his parents had in mind for him. He would be marrying into a powerful Turkish family. There would be many benefits in the alliance for not only him but for everyone in the family. So Muhammad and Shafa enjoyed their companionship and waited for the end of their closeness that could come any time. There was one stipulation that Shafa made which Muhammad accepted sadly, that he would inform her the day he had returned to his Turkish home. Distance would help her accept the finality without any complications. Shafa knew he loved her despite the fact that he never made any physical overtures to her, and she responded accordingly. Sadly enough, love often has to languish in looks and hide in a platonic relationship, unrewarded and unfulfilled.

The day before he left he met her in the hospital cafeteria where they ordered coffees and cakes. He didn't have to tell her anything to prepare her. She just knew in the way highly intuitive people know somethings. Then he was gone when the pager called and he took her hand softly and said goodbye. Then a couple of days later the phone rang from Izmir. She took the call, a very short and calm message from his mother. That surprised her. It wasn't part of the deal but she forgave him. He was from another world that did not include her nor offer her a place through adoption. Maybe it was better this way. Who knew?

The year passed slowly. Business as usual, healing the sick and the injured. She went about her work with the usual efficiency that characterized her status in the German hospital. One day there was an emergency. A radical group of international agents had been apprehended in a police raid. There had been a shoot-out. There were some wounded to see to. From her clipboard she read the details of one of them. She looked into the face of the wounded man. His graying hair, his Mediterranean features. His light gray eyes burned in her brain. There lay the man who had commanded the Sudanese bandits. She recognized him in a flash. This was the face that had been tormenting her in her nightmares. He had been responsible for the death of her brother and mother and all the innocent men, women and children. There was no Muhammad with whom to share this knowledge and advise her on the best course of action. The man's eyes momentarily flickered open. In the time that he had left he saw her but did not show any recognition. There had been far too many women and children he had killed in cold blood. He had somehow managed to swindle himself into Europe to continue the war against hated white men. There was a corrupt network of men who had acquired sufficient influence by bribery and supplying of drugs which had been spectacularly successful in infiltrating Europe with sleepers, all ready to act in any way required of them. They were evil and murderous networks.

And now she would be fighting a war of her own, one she wasn't equipped to undertake. She wondered just what should be done. The sheer weight of moral fatigue clouded her mind.

SHOUTING AT THE DEVIL

Mercy Hospital had a hospice built near it about four years ago. It was so appropriate to call it Mercy Hospice. People came here to die. Their last days were meant to be serene and comfortable as possible till they drew their last breath and the staff prepared their remains for the funeral directors to conduct the interment or cremation.

The June morning was humid and a bit chilly. Clouds rendered the world gray and forlorn. Under a red and gold Chinese tallow tree I sat on a bench set at the edge of the lawn. The grass beneath my feet was moist and soft. A wagtail hopped about snapping up anything that moved on the grass. The distant traffic could barely be heard. The wagtail and traffic flow were a reminder that life flowed on all around, and that was all death really was about. The wagtail had a nest it called home just as every vehicle had a destination, too.

Paul and Julie were our friends. They had emigrated from India some 14 years ago. They came from "good old British India stock" as Paul laughingly used to say. It was a fact. They proved they were completely culturally compatible and fitted in so well into Australian society. They were more British than Indian. They had proved excellent teachers and had given liberally to Australian children who had the good fortune of having had them for teachers. Their career had been a blessing to us.

Now Paul lay on the brink of death, wide-mouthed and of dulled eyes. I couldn't bear to see him hooked up with tubes everywhere and his chest barely heaving with weakened breath. Prayers and masses had proved inadequate to cure him of his pancreatic cancer. Eventually Julie said she accepted God's will that Paul was needed in Heaven. It was strange how delusion could be a substitute for faith when faith wasn't working. Whatever brought comfort must be a blessing of sorts. Mell couldn't be here today, having fallen in the garden a couple of days ago and been ordered to bed. She was in terrible pain, but had pleaded for me to be with Julie and take her to Mercy to share the last of life with her husband. It was a pity that Julie had never learnt to drive a car all these many years, being happy enough to let Paul take her wherever she wanted to go. She was ever the memsahib of British India. She loved it that way, being content to let Paul be the master of the household. They did things together. Where you saw one you saw the other. She and Paul lived very fulfilled lives and had been so busy being blinded by life together that they had never foreseen this awful predicament in all that time.

When we are so full of vital energy and infused with a zest for life no one ever stops to foresee disaster like Paul and Julie faced today. And all the while time's winged chariot keeps drawing near.

Then one day came the meeting with the recommended oncologist. We had left the oncologist's room in an awful daze. Paul laughed at the diagnosis as did all of us, but not without the underlying sudden cold stab of fear that never stopped growing. When we are young, happy, or at least ostensibly healthy, we are indestructible. This is not an indictment on anyone. I don't mean to sound that way. As the days became weeks and the weeks ran into a month, it became apparent that the cancer was becoming aggressive and Paul began to suffer. So did Julie. Gone were all our laughter and jokes, all our café and restaurant capers. Life had taken a somber turn. Eventually Paul had to go into hospital and then into hospice care. It all happened so quickly. It was bewildering to make any sense of it to us or to anyone, for that matter.

I soon arranged for Julie to spend as much intimate time with Paul as possible, realizing that there were desperate words that needed to be said, and assurances given. She would not want anyone to overhear her outpourings of affection and caring she would want to lavish on her dying husband, friend and lover. There were tears to be exchanged whilst they clung to each other.

We had had so many happy times together at the beach, at dinners, at cinemas, restaurants and cafes, at the footy and so many other happy occasions. It was Paul who laughed the longest and loudest and who drank the most. He was the incorrigible raconteur whose jokes were always just that little bit on the rough side as he earned the playful reprimand from Julie with a slap on the bottom. Life had been so good but fleetingly good. And now it was all drawing to a close. We never realize what lurks just around the corner. Life can be sweet one day and a bitch the next. It made no sense, really. What is the purpose of life, one has to wonder. I couldn't hold back a tear that managed to sneak away down my right cheek.

Damn! How soon it all passes away, and sometimes at such a terrible price. Why couldn't death be nothing more than that unknown, painless final sleep?

After a while I decided to creep quietly into Room 20 and share the time with Paul and Julie. Julie would need a lot of support. She had many friends and family, his and hers, who would also be there for her. They had been coming regularly and would be here again soon enough when work released them. It had been a stressful time for all.

I walked the final ten meters of a softly carpeted corridor to be hit by the sound of raised voices. I didn't know what to make of it. The noise was making its way out of Room 20. It made no sense.

I froze at the door. Julie was standing at the head of the bed and screaming.

"I've loved you every minute of our lives. How can you yell at me like this?"

Then Paul replied in a high-pitched voice that sounded nothing like his:

"I've asked you so many bloody times not to let these people into my room. I don't care who they are. All they want must be to watch me die."

"Dam you. Paul, how humiliating this is. All our lives you've been so loving and kind. Never a cross word. What the hell has got into you? Don't you realize that we all love you? And want to comfort you and share these last moments together?"

Paul emitted a short, sarcastic gasping laugh.

"Go on, get out. Let the devil take what's left of my diseased body. I can't take this any more. Let me go."

Julie screamed something back. By then I was too horrified to take note of all that they were screaming to each other, Julie through her tears and sobs and Paul through his relentless agonies.

A nurse came running into the room. She urgently ushered Julie and me out into the lounge. Another nurse had gone in with a morphine release to quieten him. They locked the door to minister to his needs in private.

My heart went out to Julie who cried inconsolably. She buried her head in my chest and sobbed and cried for some time and then I heard her say, "Why did he turn on me like that? I don't deserve it. He suddenly doesn't love me any more. He can die any time without forgiving me or giving me a chance to forgive him and convince him that I still love him as ever before. Even more so now. We need to be reconciled. What are we to do, Roger?"

I had no answer.

I took her outside to where I had been recently. I held her trembling body and couldn't deal with the repeated questions, "What have I done wrong? Why is he saying all these things, Roger? I cannot make sense of all this."

Nor could I. The chill June morning and the chill within our hearts made us numb. The wagtail sailed down from the Chinese tallow tree and landed a few feet from us. It cocked his head at us. From the roof of the hospice an ugly black crow poured its contempt at every thing mortal.

The social worker came running out to where we were. She took Julie away in an embrace. They spoke briefly and went inside. I followed. There was nothing else for me to do. I felt superfluous. One of the senior nurses came to me and asked if I needed anything. Maybe a cup of tea or coffee which I declined with thanks.

"I realize this must be very upsetting for you as well. It's been known to happen some times," she offered. I was given a brief summary of the Kubler Ross theory to help me understand what was happening to Paul but I couldn't pay close attention to any of it. Shaking all over, I went over all that had happened so unexpectedly and explosively. Nothing made sense any more.

"I know it is bewildering. But you must help her to cope. It's been traumatic for her. You should know that he wasn't really meaning to hurt her. He is a really frightened man. He hasn't long to go now. What you just witnessed and heard was Paul and Julie shouting at the devil for that is what the dying sometimes see death as. Sometimes the dying slip away with a sigh. Sometimes some shout at approaching death. It is all so final that if they are conscious of it they get very frightened. It's their way of trying to ward off the nearing specter of death. Let's find Julie. We will help her all we can, and you and her parents and friends must do the rest in the days and weeks to come."

The hospice seemed an alien place suddenly. There was a sad irony about the name "Mercy Hospice". It was a place for the dying. We had to get out from there as soon as possible. Her parents and friends were being sent for. The hospice doctor had been summoned and he came to us with a weak smile. Paul hadn't passed on. They had given him something for pain management and sleep. Decisions had to be taken as to what course the hospice should be allowed to take if he went into a coma. They were asking her to let Paul pass away. How was Julie ever to give her consent after all this had recently taken place? It smattered too much like a revenge of sorts. I shook off the thought. How ungracious it was of me. It was not what I thought of her. I knew her too well for that. But it was going to make it all the more difficult for her.

It seemed to me that all the agony and suffering was being postponed for another day. I wondered how Julie would stand up to revisiting her dying husband later that day or the next, or the next, if there was to be a next. What would happen to the happy memories? She had a lot to overcome. I hoped that nothing had begun to die within her. What we had undergone had merely been a rehearsal. They should spare Paul any more trauma and let him slip away now and escape the storm of suffering he didn't deserve, regardless of what his religion may have to say about it. Death was one human reality religions did not handle very well. They sought to deflect their inability by so-called myths that served the charade of their conceptions of reality.

Julie waited with the doctor and nurse whilst I walked to where the car had been parked. Traffic hissed past in the distance. The ebb and flow of life. The wagtail had been joined by some inquisitive magpies who might have sensed something of the human dimensions of pain and suffering. They had temporarily paused in the process of looking for food to fuel the life within them. As we drove out they renewed contact with life again. The bitter raucous sound of the black crow followed us out. It was so maddeningly derisive of human tragedy.

THE PEACOCK DANCES OVER SINJAR

Sinjar rises sharply out of the sandy wastes of the desert. It has a rocky limestone base for its foundation above which rises what is virtually a small plateau of sand, totally devoid of life, except for scorpions, lizards and snakes.

The sun is the sole guardian of the mountain, preserving it exclusively for the divine authority of the peacock goddess of death, who is believed to reside in Mt Sinjar. Some say it has been seen from time to time by travellers and those whose curiosity has taken them to the country surrounding the mountain, but never to the flat summit where the peacock danced.

The country around it is desert but blessed with a few fertile watercourses to where tribes of the mainly pastoral Yazidi people migrate from time to time to eke out their precarious living, sometimes amiably enough but sometimes also in violent resolution of tribal issues. The history of this region had not been a happy one. Though the Yazidi tribes were a warring people they looked up at Mt Sinjar with fear.

None of them went up to the summit of the mountain which over the centuries of tribal culture, they had come to accept the residence of over-arching claims of sovereignty of the peacock goddess of death and her hordes of hovering devils who could at times be seen swooping like huge black demonic bats. Those who were inquisitive enough and had to know what there was on the summit of the sacred mountain, for one reason or another, climbed to explore the mystery, were never seen again.

On one such occasion in the middle of August a steady slowly moving stream of ragged Yazidis could be seen climbing the Mount Sinjar. From afar they would have looked like a trail of ants. They were not there to solve a mystery; they were there to save themselves, which in itself was a sad irony of fate. There were no roads, so they had to follow where the leading young men picked their way between boulders and limestone faces. They tried to pick the shortest way to the summit because of the condition of the elders, the mothers and their children. Each mother carried a child. Already they had lost so many on their escape route. Death was a constant companion. This was because food and water were in very scarce supply. The heat of the mountain trail made some Yazidis reel in exhaustion and collapse. They clawed their way over huge scattered boulders to the top. They staggered, they stumbled and staggered over the rocky outcrop. Some had to be left where they fell, or were rolled over the top into the valley below to the accompaniment of the wailing and screaming of their loved ones, but the zigzagging column climbed stubbornly on and on, anxious to make their escape from their murderous enemies below who would be closing in to massacre the lot of them. They had been caught in between the butchers who sought to behead them and the bat-like demons who were said to kill anyone who invaded the sanctity of their lair, Mt Sinjar.

At the edge of the fleeing column three young men gently lowered the wicker basket which they had carried. They had temporarily abandoned the vanguard to take a rest. From out of the wicker couch came the faint and weakened wailing of an old man. A feeble hand waved about for some reason. His invocations to Yazdan, the Creator and Destroyer of of all Things, quavered through longer but weakening intermittent calls. They had carried the old man day and night, stopping only to sponge his leathery and wizened face and give him sips of water. There was no food they could offer him and so the old man grew weaker and weaker as his death approached him. He was no ordinary old man. He was the last al-Yazid, or prophet of the Kurds and their cousin ethnic cousins, the Yazidis. They shared his authority in reverence and awe. His aged eyes for the last time lit up but not for long. There in the brazen sky above him was the most beautiful azure and greenish hue filtering through the wings of the peacock god, Yazdan, who assumed the configuration of the dancing peacock before he revealed himself to that part of his world of his domination and where desolation was about to descend.

The youngest of the three guardians, Mehmet, managed to improvise some sort of crude tent to shield him from the sun which was reducing the pathetic fleeing rabble into howling and final writhings of dying and exhausted mass of what were barely human beings evading the short swift death of lethal automatic weapons instead of a slow painful and protracted dying in pain and hunger and the heat.

Babies and children, women, young and old slowly closed their eyes whilst their loved ones lay beside them crying to the Mount Sinjar for help.

The old prophet, his face barely in the shade provided by Mehmet, pointed to the fierce and brazen sky that was being consumed by the midday sun and waved his bony hands above him as if to drive off the huge black wings of the circling demons Yazdan, the Destroyer, sent to do his bidding. He had Created and now he Destroyed. But before he destroyed he revealed his ultimate creative power in his peacock image that spanned the visible earth from one end to another. There was no Destroying without Creating and there was no Creating without Destroying. The two were part of the same reality. The old man had made his final prophesy to the people before they had begun to climb Sinjar. This was where they, the last of the brave Yazidis, were meant to die. It would be a holier death at the hands of the huge black bat-like demons flying around them, than at the hands of the evil and corrupted Sunni mongrels of ISIS. Some mothers smothered or strangled their babies and children, some old and weakened ones were similarly dispatched. The circling black-winged monsters fed their insatiable appetites. Their eerie screechings rent the hot Sinjar air. The desert came to be littered with corpses spread out wherever they had been assisted to meet their death. Wailing and invocations rose and fell. The end of their world was near.

Mehmet, Abdelkadar and Mustaphar cowered near the corpse of Al Yazid. They wished they had been able to offer him a more honorable funeral with all the funeral rites a chieftain was entitled to. They cried softly to one another and wished each other a brotherly farewell. They held their weapons closer to them. Their watery and furtive eyes swept the mountain top, watching for the approach of the black flag bearers of death. They would not die alone. They would wait the approach of the humvees the IS drove. They would come drenched in the blood of the Kurd and Yazidi rear-guard action that was never destined to live for more than half a day at the most.

The old chief asked them to leave him and attend to the wounded, sick and the dying. No one moved, not wanting to leave the side of their prophet. However, with what energy he could summon up the old man shouted at his bearers to do as he commanded. His bony body was shaken with hoarse coughing. He commanded even as he lay on this accursed mountain top trying to be a leader to all.

The three young warriors were obedient unto their death. They would honor their chieftain, their last chieftain. They discussed the matter shortly. It was decided that Mehmet would stay with him. The two others went around the scattered refugees seeing how they could help them. There wasn't much that could be done. They couldn't carry their dead with them so they decided to despatch them the only way they knew how. Abdelkadar and Mustaphar rolled the dead and dying into ravines or over into the empty river courses farther below. It was a painful ordeal one they all hated but they accepted the inevitable. In time they managed to gather everyone together in a group, not that it would deter the murderous foes or even slow them down in any way.

From down below, rumbling drunkenly over the rubble and boulder-strewn track they had previously struggled to climb came the humvees with black flags flying above the guns. Battle songs from dry throats were slaked on the prospect of the imminent slaughter they were to inflict on the brethren of the Sunni faith but who recently had been proscribed as apostates and fit for the slaughter.

The humvees lurched from side to side as the wild singing of revolutionary songs tore from the throats of the animals that sought the death of those who waited to die on the top of Sinjar. Black flags flew from all the humvees, but some were carried by those who climbed afoot. They chanted as they advanced to forward positions. The cowering enemies waited their fate. The sun would set on a mountain stained with blood.

Like rabbits petrified and staring into a car's headlights they waited their deaths, the men, women and children of the Yazidis. They could run no further. The mothers gathered their children to themselves in one last final embrace of their coming death. The children cried, as did some men. They gathered at the head of their numbers to form a fragile barrier. They were determined to be the first who died. Those who had swords or daggers drew them and spent their last moments trying to sharpen the blades. One or two young warriors had some rifles. They held their guns before them, hoping to take as many of the ISIL with them. The black bats swirled and swooped and rose again in devilish screechings. If the ISIL fighters also saw them they remained unaffected and ignored the messengers of death.

Dreadful cries rose from the Yazdis men and women as their enemies poured over them. One little boy suddenly left his mother and fled in terror as fast as he could hoping to get away. His mother screamed his name and cried loudly imploring her son to return to her. He was chased by a laughing ISIL fiend with relish as he planned the most hideous end for the runaway. Those who were armed died immediately in a hail of bullets. The women and children took longer to die as the butchers went to work with their knives. This attracted the circling vultures overhead.

Further down below the crest in one final act of reckless defiance young Mahomet, Degradable and Mustard, calling the name of Allah, firing from the hip charged into the advancing column. They could no longer bear to hear the sounds of torture and rape as women died along with their children. This final desperate act of defiance proved hopelessly inadequate as it was fated to be.

A withering fire of cannon and machine guns cut them down before they even got to one hundred metres of the nearest vehicle. Soon their heads were removed from their corpses and adorned the tops of the humvees. So it was with the women and their children, too. Overhead the monstrous black bats of Yazdan dived and flew up alternatively with the image of the peacock goddess of death suffusing their world in the diaphanous peacock colours. These were the colors of evil. They revealed a world the gods forgot to love. History would record that evil triumphed in places like Mt Sinjar and no one really cared for the innocent families who fell off the face of the earth, unknown and almost as if the world did not care.

It was all over, but for the newspaper headlines of the morning papers all around the world and the TV news clips that enthralled, or nauseated, as the case may have been, breakfast viewers next day. Editors the world over had ready-made copy material over which they let their imagination run wild. Many were the stories that would be told, none with much by way of the truth.

THERE'S NO STRANGER
DANGER THAN LOVE

"My God, what on earth are you doing here?" the old lady gasped in her wheelchair.

The room was still. None of the sounds of the night intruded. It was here that she usually sat in her loneliness. She neither read the papers nor watched TV. Her amputation from life was complete. The soporific ticking of the grandfather clock could be depended on bringing much welcomed sleep early every night. The time had come to heed the summons of the clock when her lone-ness was cruelly broken. It began with the soft click of the door's lock. Slowly the door swung open. The old lady stared at the man who came in and stood staring at her. Recognition came slowly as her eyes managed to slowly focused and comprehension dawned on her and shocked her.

She gasped.

"My god, what are you doing here?"

A mixture of shock and hate flushed through her frail body. With narrowed eyes she stared through her spectacles at the intruder and recoiled with surprise, hate and horror. She tried to rise but was too weak and sank back in her wheelchair. Her emotions were in a tumultuous state and anchored her to her wheelchair. She felt a scream rising up within but bile choked it off. It left a bitter-sour taste in her mouth. As she stared, a growing fear struggled with her other outraged emotions. How could this have happened? Had fifteen years passed so quickly?

Fifteen years had indeed passed quickly for this sad, reclusive Miss Haversham. Loneliness makes the diurnal passing a veritable eternity but by way of retrospect it can seem as only yesterday. The years had also passed for one who had languished in a penitentiary, for him who had been convicted of a heinous crime, and incarcerated for the sexual assault of his ten year old niece, Sasha Harper. The case had made public history and the gossip for a whole season at least.

"Is it you?" she peered through dimming eyes. "You perverted bastard. What brings you here, you fiend from hell?" she managed, as her voice struggled with emotions that were proving too hard for her to control.

"Get out. Get out from here immediately. Or I shall call the police. How dare you come here!"

"Call the police? Isn't that how it all began some sixteen years ago which caused me to run as far as I could until my arrest and later trial? It was blind panic that drove me and blinded my reason. What never came out was hidden away in Sasha. I was never granted permission to talk to her alone for even five minutes that would have cleared the air. Without that fugitive time I was never going to answer any question, nor was Sasha ever going to talk to anyone. It was all so contrived, appearing in the court and having to answer their questions by way of well-rehearsed responses. Has she ever said a word since?"

The old woman wheeled herself as quickly as she could to the phone on the side mahogany table. She grabbed it off the cradle and began dialing. There was no response. She stared down at it. She dialed furiously again and again but with the same result. "What have you done, you swine?" she asked with some alarm as it dawned on her that he must have cut her off from the outside world.

He hadn't moved. The gaunt, hollow-eyed man breathed laboriously, chest heaving slightly as one who was under some stress, or recovering from hard labor. He didn't take his eyes off the old woman who had now broken out in a sweat, and fear opened her eyes wide so that she could sit staring at him.

When he spoke he sounded as if he had a sore throat and he struggled with words and coughed intermittently.

In a tired voice he said he knew that neither she nor his sister, Ruth, would ever be satisfied unless he was still in gaol and would stay in gaol to rot slowly in that hell and never to be released. His fifteen years had indeed been a lifetime in hell, during which he had been beaten up by other prisoners many times in the yard, in the gym, in the dining room and heaven knew where else he had lost recollection of. He had been tortured and raped. He had died within himself slowly so that when they eventually one day told him that he was to be discharged he felt no elation. He had come out of Pentridge into the harsh light of day with a small suitcase with the pathetically few possessions he still had which he could call his own.

The encounter with the free world filled him with a terrible fear. Every shadow, every nightfall was peopled with monsters and heart-stopping panic. Ever so slowly in the nights and days ahead his confidence returned. It took him some time to learn how to deal with the outside world again. So much had changed just as he had. He no longer startled at shadows or when a stranger spoke to him. Eventually he managed to land a job with a work crew repairing sections of rutted roads. He earned his own wages with an honest job. A new identity was shaping up in him, but for all that the fugitive life was ever close by. He felt that he could no longer read a newspaper. He no longer trusted them to print the truth about him. The tragic figure of a former self never faded away completely. There was still a passionate desire to prove himself an honest man, one who had been terribly wronged. Sometimes he felt he wouldn't bother. He would let life unfold as it took its course. It was enough for him to cope from one day to another.

The day came when a small voice with all its quiet but insistent promptings urged him to try and return to what once had been his home. In order to do this he would need to begin from where his former life once ended. He had to see Sasha again. His mother had to know what had transpired in those awful days of his arrest, trial, conviction and incarceration. She had to believe him even if no one else ever did. There would be one other who knew he was innocent of all he had been charged with. The fact that he had been found guilty, sentenced and convicted in a court of law did not make him guilty. The guilt lay with society; the guilt lay with those who had stage-managed his imprisonment. They did not want justice, he realized; they wanted a result. The system had to be vindicated. It was all they cared about. There had been far too many child-molestations. This disease had to be incised like some malignant cancer. Other children and their parents needed to keep faith in the legal system and to retain a sense of confidence that they were being protected and that there was no way out for the guilty monsters, pedophiles.

Sasha knew the truth. He needed to see her. She loved him still. He believed it with all his heart. She had become a young woman. He had a better opportunity now to see her. But first he had to set things right with his mother. It wasn't going to be easy, he could see that. He had been warned to keep away from them all or he would serve out the fullest term of his sentence. But first he had to put things right with his mother, before she passed away. It meant so much to him. Now he was here, alone with her, but with her believing in his guilt.

The old woman sat with the phone dangling from her hand. She looked up at him. How pale he had become. An unhealthy pallor was spread across his face. The color of the leper's skin, she mused quietly. Hate now mingled with a genuine sense of fear. What was he going to do? Would he kill her? His eyes seemed to now be mere slits, and darting from side to side furtively like the eyes of a lizard. She feared for her life…and, yet, she was his mother. Surely it would deter him. Surely he wouldn't kill her? She looked at him differently after a time. She might be able to forgive him, to release him of his anger.

She didn't find it easy to focus. Her mind for some reason drifted away to the time when he was her little boy. So innocent and so loving. He loved running errands for her. Through his school years he would bring his little sporting awards to her to show her and win her admiration. It mattered to him. She had to reach that little and lovable boy somehow. But how? She wondered if he retained any of that love for her. That love was all that could save her now, she feared.

Her head slumped to her chest as she said, "What are you going to do?" She nearly uttered the word "son" but bit her lip in time. No. That son died a long time ago after his trial when everything that was a series of distortions came out. No matter how hard she tried to put that behind her she struggled to see him anew but first she had to be able to forgive him.

"You want to know what I am going to do, mother? Nothing! I don't know what you expect me to do because you have let me know, let me feel what you think of me. All I want to do now is to tell you, whether you and the rest of the poisonous tribe believe me or not, is that you have destroyed me and taken away what was and is the most precious things in life, innocence and honor.

Sasha knows what I say is the truth and that is all that matters to me. She was never called to testify. She was never questioned even after she said that she wanted to. Tell her when you see her next all I have said this day. Tell her I may run into her one day and we will, as adults, put matters right because now no one can get at her..."

Her voice cut him off sharply, "No. Keep away from her. Give her a chance to get along with her life, to put the worst behind her. That takes a life time."

"No one can get at her, the child that once was. The past is past. She is no longer inaccessible to me nowadays since her parents have passed away. Hah! Why doesn't it make me grieve for them? Hopefully Sasha would have got over her loss perhaps.

You may never forgive me for what you believe I went to prison for but for the last time, mother, let me say it was all delusional and I have been punished for nothing. I am still an innocent son of yours. I shall try and get by and make a life for myself. OK, I'll be in touch from time to time to see how you are."

His mother's frame shuddered at the prospect. A sob rent her body.

"One day your eyes may yet open to the truth, if you care to search earnestly for it. Begin with talking to Sasha. Good bye. Find peace, mother."

The last he saw of her was a shattered old woman in a wheel chair, head fallen on her slowly heaving chest with a telephone in her hand, the cut cord dangling hopelessly. That is sadly just how love suffers sometimes. Cut off from the truth and reconciliation.

Mother. Sasha.

Sasha!

Where was she now? Happy, he hoped. Perhaps married.

It was too late for me to make my re-appearance in her life. If you really love someone then it may be better to do nothing that may upset the person's peace and happiness – and, yes, what was once a love. It is true.

There's no stranger danger than love.

THE DAY THE RAINS CAME

Our destinies on this earth are thought to be in our own hands, or at least, so we have been urged to believe to inspire us to make us live fruitful lives. But every now and then we come to be confronted by an insensate earth that fully challenges us by the deadly storms at sea, the earthquakes of heaving convulsive earth and the consequences of prolonged periods of drought.

Close to the borders of southern Queensland and northern New South Wales in an area that floods have frightened off insurance brokers or invited them to invent exorbitant premiums to cover flood damage in what is generally regarded as the wide flood plain in that stricken part of Australia. Often as not it is seasons of unrelenting drought that transform farmlands into dust bowls.

And that is where the story is set, in and around the rural town of Carradarra, NSW. There came a drought one year that reduced the land to bare hard-baked and cracked earth. Where once there were trees, bushes and what were once crops, there were now sad, dead, brown wasted remains of vegetation in a sepia land of human misery that filled the eyes and hearts of everyone who knew and cared. It had become a land without pity or hope. There was nothing unusual in that. These fate-hardened people knew the suffering these conditions brought in their wake. It makes one wonder why they should take the trouble to keep returning to their nightmares when their ordeals had passed.

One no longer looked into another's face in case he saw a devastation worse than the one he had tried to hide from his neighbours. It would have made their fears grow into panic looking into their faces of the coming doom. There were many who trembled at what they felt was their end gradually unfolding. It wasn't easy to confront the fearful prospect. It made one wonder what God thought of them. There were no prayers rendered to him that he hadn't heard before, many times before, in fact.

Prayer is the last resort of the faithless even if it may be the first resort of the devotees. The church and Hindu temple of Carradarra began to fill up in an uncharacteristic manner. The priests called all the faithful to pray every day of the week. They prayed so earnestly for rain. The priest of St Andrew's church promised them, in the name of God, that they would be rewarded if they opened their hearts and purses. God became the happy recipient of greater wealth than hither to. Whilst God was a god of love and mercy, they were his children whose gratitude had to be expressed in the generosity of the blessed children of God. He would hear their prayers. Whatever you asked in his name he would do or give. The priests seized the opportunity to remind them it came at a price.

It was a time when every one knelt and fervently sent up prayers in a petition to God. The priest from the altar assured them that he had heard the voice of God. Rain was on its way. But nothing happened. Cloudless skies still smiled heartlessly down on their world. The following week still nothing. Anxious eyes searched the horizons for any hint of coming hope. The earth baked hard. Cracks ran along the earth. Trees and bushes that had struggled to survive so far began to wilt and run to ochre, yellow or brown hues as they slowly died off. The days became furnaces and no one ventured outside for any length of time. The sun's rays baked the human skin and made the exposed areas leathery. Perspiration ran in rivulets except in air-conditioned buildings which was why the shopping centre was congested because of the number of poor took refuge from the heat, but the heat found them out after hours when they had to return to baking homes.

By the end of the month only the sick and very old came to church and tried to keep their intercessionary prayers going. Hope in the hearts of the others began to fade into derision that indicated the collapse of faith. Then one afternoon a group of excited sky-watchers pointed to a dark line forming over the horizon. It grew into a smudge. The appearance of extra terrestrial crafts couldn't have created greater excitement. The grey smudge soon grew in larger and larger proportion.

Clouds?

The word sped through the town. The word sped through all the farms. The word sped through to the next town. And to the next and so on. Many ran out on to the streets. Some fell on their knees and cried. Soon the churches were full again. Faiths of the faithless were re-ignited. The priest urged them to keep up the pressure on God in case he relented and scattered the clouds away. So hymns were sung with great passion and prayers were shouted. And the first sprinkles drew children into the streets with their dogs and cats, and they danced and sang in the streets and fields and their fathers joined them as the rain fell harder. Mothers called to them to come back and get dry or they would get sick, but all in vain.

They resigned their efforts and decided that they may as well join them. There was a great deal of rejoicing and frivolity in the streets. Dirty but happy they later bathed in what they hailed as their new-found rescue.

The priest was feted as their intercessionary saviour. Whenever he and wherever he went about he was loudly hailed and cheered. The publicans shouted him free beers. He was their hero. He loved the attention. God be praised for he had heard their prayers and was giving them what they had prayed for. Their hour of deliverance was at hand as had been promised.

The clouds opened and thunder of fulfilling promises came repeatedly crashing down. Then the rains fell harder. Lightning came as reproof of what had been their flagging faith. In time it was so heavy that those driving cars began to crash into each other as visibility was soon almost down to a mere metre. The river finally overflowed its banks and the streets became a torrent. Branches of trees and bushes came swirling down in the rivers of destruction. The people were soon back in church, this time more fearfully. Fields became a sea of brown waters and churned up the soil. It was feared that the fields, if the flood remained for a greater length of time, would not bear any crops for many months to come. They would become bogs. Farmers faced ruin and repossession of their homes and stock.

In some streets cars were seen floating by in hot pursuit of white goods that floated past. Soon houses weakened and were torn off their pads as they joined in the mad race in the swirling torrent that sped past at a fearful gathering speed. Householders made pathetic pictures as they were seen clinging to their homes, some waving out for someone to assist them in arresting their movement in the swirling progress of the turgid, brown torrent. The town's policeman had run from one place to another trying to assist people. It would later be said that he saved many from drowning. At least three little ones were pulled from the raging rivers of silt and returned to overpowered mothers who could not find the strength to do any more. They cried out to those they knew and even to those who may have been strangers but had become witnesses to their suffering. No one, however, could be of any help. Each was alone in his helplessness. Each was too absorbed in his own loss.

Church attendance fell away sharply again. Some said God had a sick sense of humor. Father told remaining worshipers that God had sent them the rain they had prayed for but it was also as a test of their faith. He loved them and was only testing this faith. If he didn't love them he would not have used the rain to give them an opportunity to prove their trust. Everything was going to be all right, but unfortunately for all his powers of persuasion he couldn't explain why Mrs Murphy lost her three month baby in a surge of brown muddy death or why the 80 year old widow was swept out of her house, gone forever. Before the waters began to subside twenty one people had perished in the floods. Those who had survived could be seen counting their losses. Men and women sobbed and cried, their children added to the sound of disaster by their frightened wailing. In the background and rising above the sounds of human misery could be heard the heavy roaring of the flood waters.

Gradually, long after the survivors had been reduced to a shambles of their former selves the rains eased off, the flood waters remained but as reduced swirling bodies of debris-filled disaster. People came out diffidently as if they did not trust to the abatement of the flood. They looked about agonizingly, painfully as they called out to those they recognized, some who might have been neighbours, some who were their work-mates. There wouldn't be any work now for anyone to bring them together again. They met and exchanged news about their losses and commiserated with each other. Never was comradeship better experienced and shared.

Shared misfortunes and experiences of disaster bring people closer than they ever were before and they experience again the best of their humanity as they try to help each other. The other man's grief and loss are added to their own. Women give friends and lovers a strength they never knew they had and they smiled through their wet and browned faces. Children clung to their parents afraid to be ever separated again.

There were only two funerals. The other bodies were reduced to what had become boggy graves without the benefit of prayers and blessings. Corpses were being found periodically sometime later, some at a distance from where they lived. The bereaved didn't want to see the priest ever again. God had become their killer; their tormentor. They not only had lost all their faith but they no longer believed there was a benevolent God who loved them and promised to look after them. Those who still clung to him saw God as one to be feared. He had promised to answer their prayers, instead he was destroying his children, as they had once been taught to see themselves. He no longer had any credibility. God was a punishing god, a god of death and destruction. Some drew historical parallels of an emerging truth - he was responsible for every war that had ever been fought. After a short break still the rains continued to fall, sometimes growing in unabating strength. Storms picked up in strength and drove people farther away from one they had worshipped as God.

It was no longer safe for the priest to go any place where death had struck a family. He was no longer welcome back in the pub. Those who still managed to respond to years of brainwashing still turned up to church but the collection plate went back with a coin or two. They no longer stayed back to thank him for his sermon. No one had a kind word for him. They passed him in the streets and looked the other way. No one looked him in the eyes or smiled appreciatively. One Sunday morning the people discovered that the church had gone, swept away with the homes of others. No one saw the priest again. It didn't make any one happy. No one really cared one way or another that they no longer had a priest. Where the church once stood was now an empty building pad littered with smashed timber pieces and odd bits of cloth, and pews in wild disarray. Where faith had once been celebrated was now a big emptiness that matched the emptiness in their souls. What was seen now and then floating down the main street turned out to be clothes that had floated in from somewhere; they could have been bed or table linen. The old wooden crucifix was seen trapped in a roll of wire with a helpless god looking about him for release. It seemed to strike an ironic image. "He came to save others but himself he could not save."

The day the rains came it restored people to their senses.

THE EGYPTIAN TAXI DRIVER

The campus was overflowing with students who moved at leisurely pace with files secured in arms crossed against their chests or in brief cases and bags. Some were very young, just out of school. Many excitedly texted their friends and parents, their eyes widening with the delivery of gossip or recounting stories of how the classes went for them. For many it was the dizzy taste of growing up in another world other than boring old school. They felt release in their new sense of accepted responsibility. Many realized that now was beginning a setting down of the foundations of the future life. Then there were the excited ones who spoke rapidly with their friends telling each other about their "awesome" new world of tertiary education. Some merely gossiped in the manner of the vacuous. They discussed their lecturers, some of whom they felt were simply gorgeous and some were just dags. They felt quite grown up suddenly. The girls, being still girls, giggled a lot, the boys inclined to be a bit sluggish with their responses, not sure of what they should be feeling. Nearly all made their ways to the students' cafe.

There were many who were in their second or third year. They had seen all this before and kept aloof, some a bit disdainful of the freshman excitement and chatter. These had long since become aware of the serious side to university life; they had other things on their minds, like the prospects of failing or the need to procure funding to keep them afloat for at least another year. They scanned notices on the Student Union notice boards, jotting down telephone numbers. Stress began to build up. Even when they laughed there was some falseness in the sound. There was suddenly somethings that had to be taken seriously. It was common knowledge that some took refuge in drugs and alcohol. The victims of substance abuse were easily detectable, it was sad to say.

Sharing the world of academia were those one couldn't miss, the gray- haired men and women who carried satchels and wore frowns. These walked more slowly. Some carried schedules in files. When in pairs they chatted seriously and thoughtfully. These were the lecturers. Some were occasionally met by students who chatted for a while till the students had the answers they needed and then took their leave and went on their way.

No one looked to be in need of more urgent haste than Dr Baker from the School of Psychology. With long and hurried strides he crossed a lawn and made his way to where a woman, Laura, his wife, and their ten year daughter, Chloe, waited. Chloe detached herself from her mother's side and ran to her father with a happy wave. She loved the atmosphere of campus. It made her feel she was growing up and she would one day be big and a university student, too. She couldn't wait, she thought, for the time to come. It was special to have one's Dad being a professor. He was special and by association so was she.

"Sorry, darling, I was held up at the last moment seeing to department needs. The opening is always chaotic, as you well know," he said apologetically, as he gave her a hug and a kiss. He didn't leave Chloe out, much to her delight.

His wife understood the problem only too well being a school teacher herself. She had a migraine coming on. At least she didn't have to go looking or waiting for Chloe, who had turned up on time outside her classroom. Together they made it to Murdoch University where they usually stood around when waiting for Dr Baker which had usually been the case judging from other years. It had now become a routine. Dr Baker ushered them into a taxi that had slid up to them, having been sent by a friend who also lectured in Psychology.

Before letting them get in Dr Baker poked his head into the front seat door and asked to see the driver's ID. This was accomplished smoothly and courteously and, thanking the driver who was one of those foreign migrants trying to eke out a living in their new country. Dr Baker then helped them into the taxi and gave the driver an address in Rocking ham.

"What's that? I'm sorry I didn't hear, darling. Oh, it's ok. No. No. He is an Egyptian, Abu Khaleed, who has started working the shifts at the university now days. I won't be later than 7 pm, I shouldn't think. I'll phone before setting out, OK?" Chloe always hated this last bit whenever he was going to be delayed at the office, but accepted it reluctantly, always making a sad face at him. With this the taxi pulled away and soon joined the Kwinana Freeway making its way in an orderly passage in a secure line of south bound traffic.

Laura had noticed the gray-green eyes of the Egyptian taxi driver. She estimated he had to be at least fifty years of age, seeing the gray flecks in his hair and beard which was ample and squarish as seemed to be the fashion of Muslim males of a certain age. She noted his beaded and colorful cap he wore. As if he sensed this show of mild curiosity the driver turned his head slightly and smiled briefly. It was a sad and slow smile of someone rather lost or at least far away in his thoughts. The moment had interrupted his quiet chanting. She had no idea what it all meant. Then she heard his voice, low and somewhat guttural.

"And how are you and your daughter, madam? I am sorry I hadn't asked earlier," he said looking in front.

Laura Baker allowed the inquiry to rest a few seconds before replying with an uncertain smile. "Oh, we are very well, thank you, driver," she said, accenting the "driver" part to establish the desired relationship. It was lost on the taxi driver.

For a while the cab hummed away efficiently and on either side the movement of cars and trucks either pulled away ahead or dropped back for a time, but the turgid flow was irrevocable as ever. At least there was an absence of recklessness as there hadn't been any crashes so far.

The taxi driver carried on with his low-pitched chanting.

He was no longer driving down the highway. His mind was not on his driving, although he had never had an accident. He was always so careful, but there were times his heart found him far away and back in those heady days of Tahrir square and the excitement of anti-Muslim Brotherhood demonstrations. The flares, the chanting, the impassioned cries of defiance, the passion. The young women he and his sons brushed shoulders with were so bold and exciting. And suddenly it was all over. He buried his sons. His wife never recovered and had to be sent to live the rest of her life with her people in Luxor. He was smuggled out to Athens where he found it possible to get papers and was successful in meeting the requirements to get visa papers for Australia. All that part of his story was never revealed to anyone, not even his best friends in his new country. But he knew he could never return to his beloved Egypt, his heaven on earth. He sang the romantic songs of his youth, songs his sons loved to sing with their beautiful voices.

He felt nostalgic tugs at his heart as he thought of those days when he could dress in his favourite galabiyya and stroll with friends on the side walks of Cairo stopping here and there to taste the delicious ta'miyya and cinnamon tea. How wonderfully relaxing it was to sit at one of his favourite cafes and smoke a hookah and discuss the politics of the world. There was so much happening that produced animated discussions with students and socialites alike. Such was life in Cairo, till all came to be lost so suddenly in the calamities created by the Muslim Brotherhood and the army that ended in the fumes of tear gas and the hurt of rubber bullets.

All that Laura Baker could remember were the occasional "Alaha hu Akbar" chanted reverently. Chloe looked up at her mother after nudging her briefly. She whispered to her mother that the Egyptian taxi driver was singing his prayers. The driver might have heard her because he stopped the soft and slow chanting. Looking straight ahead he said, "You know, madam, it is written in the Quran that it is a man's duty to respect and protect woman."

Laura wondered what this had to do with driving them to Rockingham but didn't say anything, deciding to let the words slide past. She looked into the rear view mirror and found his eyes on them for a while before darting away, surprised at being thus detected.

"I have lost all the women in my life. The soldiers came and killed all while I was away in Tahrir Square that day. I came home to find my wife and mother in the hallway. Upstairs I came across the corpses of my two daughters," he lamented, shaking his head, and saying something in Arabic. He found it expedient to tell his stories. It was useful to elaborate on them. He was a dreamer, poet and a singer. He found it wasn't too difficult to get respect and sympathy here in this country untouched by fury and revolutionary madness. It was so refreshingly different. But ah, for the longing for the palm lined main social thoroughfares of Cairo, the cafes and university cultural festivities!

Chloe nudged her mother gently again and keeping her head straight as she could to prevent the appearance of whispering to her she said, "He's crying." Laura Baker felt a sob choke her at that moment. This was an involuntary act of loss and suffering the man had to live with every moment of his life here in Australia. She wondered how he managed to get here. She wondered if he was here legally. There has been so much said in the media about illegal refugees, yet here was someone who surely deserved asylum. His losses were heartbreaking even to people like Laura Baker and her daughter.

A new sound built up in the silence that followed. They were near Rowley Road. They were nearly home. This had been a strange and unique journey into the shattered life of pain, loss and destitution. She longed to tell her husband the story, but no one else. She would ask her daughter to keep the whole incident secret. It was too intimate and they had been privileged to share a stranger's grief and pain. This had to be respected. It had become their duty to protect the tragedy from others' eyes because to broadcast it would be to betray a stranger's act of involuntary trust. Here was a suffering he couldn't keep down but needed to share it with some he trusted and laid upon them the sacred duty to share his grief and keep it sacred, not the subject of scuttlebutt and gossip. Whatever he thought of his passengers he felt honor and acceptance. Why this should be so he had no idea nor would Laura Baker and her daughter. This is a rare occasion when strangers no longer remain strangers. There is a mystical unity that binds human beings who are strangers to each others but not really all that strange if one stops to think about it.

Lara allowed herself another look at the Egyptian taxi driver. Something about the man was beginning to fascinate her. The mystery of his suffering, a re-examination of her attitude to all illegals, as she and her friends called them, the haunting look in his gray-green eyes and the hard etched pain lines that creased his cheeks and forehead and his browned skin burnt into his face by the Egyptian sun. She became concerned by his sly gaze, but something new had come to replace it. His fingers had set up a drumming on the steering. The further they went, the closer they got to Rockingham, the harder the beats came till both mother and daughter's concerned grew and they became more concerned and looked at each other. Suddenly the drumming stopped. And they heard him again.

"The Quran says it is the duty of every man to respect and defend woman. Such is the command of Allah. But no one had protected my wife and daughters."

There was a finality about the way he said it. By now the tears had dried up, but his eyes remained like portals opening into the private hell into which he spent his time looking as if he half hoped to find those he loved and lost.

They reached home at long agonized last and Laura Baker opened the door and let Chloe in. By the time she had her purse open and rummaged around to get the exact fare she heard the taxi come to life and pull away. She ran down the drive calling out to him to take his fare but all she saw was the taxi turning the corner of the neighboring street.

THE HANGING MAN

Gorgons Head was an irregular feature of the country that rose sharply some fifty kilometres off the Vasse Highway. It was a granite outcrop that was covered by dense forest except for the north face that looked down on the little bush town of Gorgonbiddie which in more prosperous times gave domicile to forest workers and their families. At the time it had a population of about three hundred altogether. The town had a pub and what was left of a motel of sorts, a church, a primary – middle school, a service station a bakery, a miniature Coles shopping centre, a newsagents that also served as a funeral parlour and a tiny Methodist church that couldn't have accommodated more than thirty worshipers. Thirty cabins had been constructed for the forest workers by South West Forest Solutions many years ago. They were now converted into B&B for young hikers mainly apart from the healthier and more adventurous older counterparts who came that way when they did the Bibulmun track now and then.

Gorgonbiddie School offered a modest and basic education to about seventy eight children of all grades. It was difficult to keep a regular staff because no one wanted to stay. The Principal was an old man. He was seldom seen about the place. One of the students in school was Chester Brodie, an obese ten year old who was very irregular in his attendance as his teacher, Mrs Barton, kept reporting to the Principal and the Brodies. Dad was never at home regularly being a FIFO worker at Mount Tom Price. Chester was the only child and was badly spoilt as is often the case. His mother had no idea what to do about his truancies. He very rarely did any work having a pronounced aversion to school. There were no social workers at the school who could help him and his mother to cope. Consequently he grew up with little or no life skills and no self-esteem but an eccentric nature that fed on a wild uncontrollable imagination.

One Friday in May Chester left home for school. He had a consumptive school bag that contained his i-pad, gym gear and a cut lunch he himself had put together. The cut lunch consisted of two sandwiches of peanut butter and a packet of cigarettes. He rarely got to school. He usually met a mate, Albert Crabapple, on the way and was easily persuaded to give school a miss and hang out at Coles and check out the chicks. That day they decided to pack it in at about five o'clock and return home.

For some reason Chester took such a long way home that it passed the foot of the disused quarry that fell away half a kilometer from the start of the forest. He was soon making his way through a complex growth of bushes, she oaks and wild gums. The footpath was quite clearly defined so he never had a problem. He loved the waist- high shrubbery and low swinging branches. In a short time he found the forest getting darker as most of the sunlight found it hard to penetrate the interior. But he wasn't scared, not here in this forest with which he had become quite familiar. Life however had a way of catching one unprepared and introducing a measure of terror into an otherwise familiar environment, even in one's home. On this occasion he had proved more wayward than usual and realized he was lost. Here was territory that he had never before explored. He realized that he was farther from the well-beaten path than he had wanted to be. Everything was so new now. He began to worry.

He very nearly banged into it. One moment he was examining the quaint behavior of a crow and the next it was there dangling from a branch square in the way. It gave him quite a turn. It appeared to be pecking at something. He let out a stifled shout. It was a hanging man, naked as the day he was born. His eyes were protruding in a hideous way and his tongue was sticking out. The body had a greenish pallor. The man would have been about the same age as dad. Chester quickly stepped smartly into some thorny undergrowth where he stayed for the time he could satisfy his curiosity. A breath of forest air hit the hanging man and slowly swung him around. Chester looked about and found what he had been looking for, a length of switch without a lot of leaves. He broke it off. Armed with it he approached the corpse cautiously in case the corpse should somehow jump down and come at him. But what was absurd, he told himself, was to find the guts for what he planned. His courage seemed to have deserted him. He cautiously approached the hanging man and whacked him a couple of times. The body turned and those bulging eyes stared directly into his own. He gulped. Next he looked for and found a rock and threw it at the corpse. It made a sickening hollow thud. Chester then suddenly began running and didn't stop till he reached home, all out of breath. Mum was hanging out the washing and jumped at the noisy entrance Chester made as he banged open the door and barged in, breathing hard all the while.

"There's a dead man hanging from a tree!" he blurted out, gulping for air as he made the announcement.

"What ever are you on about, Chester? And I bet you haven't been to school all day. I'll soon get a call summoning me to see the Principal again," his mother said menacingly.. "This time your Dad can go. What is this about a hanging man? You must be seeing things. Haven't we told you the forest is off limits to you?"

"He's swinging from a tree butt-naked," the boy added.

Mother gasped. "And you had time to stare, I suppose, instead of looking away and then running home."

"I couldn't find his clothes anywhere. But I saw his willy," he added, wide-eyed.

His mother let out a gasp. "You never!"

"Yep, I sure did," continued a determined Chester not to be done out of his dramatic discovery, thinking this was the best way to gain attention. "And it was bigger than Dad's, too."

His mother blushed and ran into the next room from where she exploded wildly, "I don't believe this. And when the hell did you ever see..." but she couldn't finish her sentence. She was too embarrassed to confront her son just then, but eventually she would have to and that sooner than later. "When Dad flies in again you can tell him this," she said.

They were all going to have a serious family discussion, that was for sure. She didn't know how that would go down. She dreaded to think about it. In the mean time something had to be done immediately. Like informing the police.

That's where the trouble began after she phoned the police. The call wasn't being treated seriously and she thought she heard the policeman snigger away from the phone. She let him know this wasn't good enough. She was going to make a report about how her report had been handled.

There was an instant change of attitude after this and the police car drove up to the Brodie residence. A Senior Constable got out of the car and sauntered up to the front door and rang the bell. He introduced himself, Senior Constable Hector Pope, and invited the mother and son to accompany him to the station to formalise the statement and get all the details he would need to find the corpse. Senior Constable Pope bundled little Chester Brodie and his mother into a police car and drove into that part of the forest where the lad claimed to have seen the hanging man.

After several failures to locate the hanging man it was understandable that both Senior Constable Hector Pope and Mrs Brodie were getting not only sceptical, but more importantly, irritated. She kept apologizing to the Senior Constable and giving Chester more than just a bit of her mind. Every now and then the lad would excitedly point to some imaginary landmark and urge the policeman to stop whilst they looked about but always to no avail.

They drove back in sullen silence. The mother hugely embarrassed, Senior Constable Pope by now irascible and Chester Brodie arms folded across his chest still spotting likely places but by now being given short shrift. Mother and son were promised a lift back in the police car but only after Senior Constable Pope preached the likely consequences of wasting police time. He kept looking at the mother to make his point. Once back at the station the Senior discovered there were three visitors waiting for him.

They were Mr and Mrs Gospel and little Mark. They were frowning and in great earnest as they hemmed in the poor and very tired policeman. Mark and Chester greeted each other perfunctorily with no more than a "Hi!", both being from Gorgonbiddie School where they weren't really the best of friends, belonging as they did to different gangs.

"Yes, what can I do for you?" asked Senior Constable Pope in his best confronting manner.

Mr Gospel spoke for them, "We are here to report the death of a man. According to Mark, there is a man hanging from a tree in the forest near by."

An awkward silence occurred before a minute later after which there was an angry explosion from the policeman.

"Very funny! Let me tell you it is an offense to waste police time. I should book the lot of you. Now why don't the lot of you call it a day and piss off and leave me alone, or it won't only be one man hanging from a tree! Go on, go home," he said, brushing off the remonstrating Mr and Mrs Gospel.

Long after the whole incident, residents of Gorgonbiddee were still known to scour the forest looking for the hanging man. There were also picnic parties to commemorate the mystery. Mark and Chester enjoyed a brief popularity as people sought them for more clues, but all to no avail.

The story should have ended here after investigations. The two boys had clearly been delusional but were later recovering well enough to continue wagging school and proving the nuisances they had previously been as ever before much to the relief of the school authorities. As long as "the hanging man syndrome had been put to bed" as the Principal so poetically put it everything was running as normal.

Until one day in rainy June Senior Constable Pope was driving through hanging man territory as the region had been named when out of the corner of his eye he caught sight of something suspended from a tree top. He braked sharply, swore aloud, reversed off the track that worked as a bit of a road and pulled up ten metres from what was clearly the stark butt naked torso of the hanging man all over again.

Senior Constable Pope wondered how he was best going to handle this. He would have to call in the regional office who had had enough dealing with the media of the previous hanging man episode. He swore some more as he headed back to the station. Here some more bad news waited for him. Constable Alice Cooper came out shuffling some papers in her hands while she came up to him and murmured,

"The Brodies and Gospels waiting to see you, Senior..." she got no further.

"Not now, Constable. Not now," Senior Constable Pope growled. "I have to make an appointment to see Dr Jung, Police Psychological Services a.s.a.p. After all this goings-on I need to see the shrink myself. Ring regional and tell someone there I will have my report written by next week. I'll leave it on my desk, OK? No. Don't ask. And while you're on the go, send those bloody spooks home after you've taken down whatever they have to say. Or I'll probably... shoot the lot of them in self-defense. There, thanks. I owe you one, doll."

He thought he had better make another visit to that part of the road where he had seen the hanging man and then he he would return to the station, go into his office to make the call.

THE SIRANGI PLAYER
OF SAGO LANE

We had returned to Singapore after an absence of some twenty years. So much had changed. More elegant condos for those who could afford them. The highly ornamental freeway into the city. Every kilometer landscaped with red, mauve and orange bougainvilleas and multi-hued and elegantly green shaped hedges, all adding to the aesthetic appeal that was Singapore. The taxi ride into the central business district was a delight. Before we knew it we were had arrived at Clark Quay. We have a passion for Clark Quay and The Mandarin Court hotel which is home for us when we are in Singapore.

Milly and I hurriedly checked into the Swissotel Merchant Court Hotel, and after a shower and some coffee we headed into Chinatown. Singapore is a city state of many moods each generated by ethnic diversity and the accompanying magic. Modernity verges on ultra-modern which itself is suddenly absorbed into Singapore's sudden contrasting mood which is traditional and reflecting a past, an older and exotic world. We wasted no time getting re-acquainted with the island state. The excitement was palpable. The whole island is alive and throbbing with excitement. At least for us it was. For Milly and me, there's no place in the world that holds such quixotic charm.

Many years ago the Chinese had built a very beautiful temple and each subsequent year something new was always added to it embellishing it and adding a colorful splendid look. It showed how devoted the Buddhists were to their Buddha. China Town had become enriched with the addition of the highly ornate Temple of The Buddha Tooth in the very heart of the district. We happily breathed in the quixotic spice-laden air.

The Singaporeans don't do things by halves. This was once The Street of The Dead. It had originally housed the hospice for poor Chinese where relatives could buy candles, joss sticks, funeral cloths and cheap coffins. Not that there weren't dying poor Chinese anymore in the new affluent Singapore, but now they were now obliged to die somewhere else out of sight. There was a disturbing lack of compassion in the new world here. The suave and slick materialism was breeding something new; a losing sight of the human. A modernity was replacing the best of the traditional past we loved. It was what kept drawing us back to experience, a lost world of a different elegance and magic.

Much of old Chinatown had been demolished in 1961 and a carefully planned new heart was built in 1972. This was a sort of commercialization of death in the new Singapore. Perhaps I am being a bit too critical, maybe even a bit envious of the island state, I don't know. Maybe. But the current landscape was a strange admixture of lovely modern towering complexes that formed a backdrop of the ultra-modern commercial world of affluence. Against this was set the lovely quintessential Chinese old world architecture. Past and present had learnt to co-exist in a happy compromise, as yet. But there were disturbing scenes, nevertheless. We felt we were sort of intruders.

Shamelessly we sort of did the touristy thing. We gawped around the place to satisfy the eyes, ears and nose as we drank in the charm of Sago Street and the new temple. I wandered about peering at all the things for which the natives were shopping. Milly loved the trinkets and baubles, often exclaiming her delight and imploring my attention. I tend not to get too excited except when I know it would please her. Then I would oblige with a supporting "ooh!" or an "aah!" She could spend many hours sampling all the shops and ruining our holiday budget, in the bargain!

We loved brushing shoulders with the teeming masses especially in China Town and Little India. Serrangoon Road is a very special part of Singapore. We picked our way through the shopping crowd that day near the Buddhist temple. This was when I heard the quaint and, what I thought, somewhat disordered strain of stringed music. I ignored it for a little while but wherever I turned it was there. It was a quaint, stringy sound producing a sort of plaintive melody that was new to us. Milly held my arm and asked me if I could detect from where the music was emanating. We searched all about the place eagerly. She looked behind her once and pointed out the sirangi player who sat on a low stool. The sirangi was a poor, crude-looking two-string musical instrument which was played with a bow. For a moment only did it totally absorb us. Then the sirangi player caught our attention.

Our sirangi player, to all outward appearances was an ancient, toothless, yellowing ancient Chinaman whose desiccated and wrinkled skin gave him the appearance of an animated relic whose skin was as old as parchment. He obviously enjoyed what he was doing, playing his music for his world to listen to. So we paid him the tribute of what was intended to be a five minute audience. He appreciated it because he smiled all the more. This exposed the toothless gap that was meant to be a smile. We smiled back. We enjoyed the interlude. So, too, did he. He was part of the music as much as the music was a part of him. It touched a part of me that made my trip to Singapore an event whose memory would always be cherished in a very special way. My sirangi player and his music meant more than I would have been able to put into words at the moment if anyone asked me to. We hadn't planned for the length of time we became his audience. I have thought about the old musician many times after that. This seemed to be where past and present met. It was seamless. Time ceased to exist for us. Then he did more than just play his sirangi; he looked at us.

At that moment I felt that his wise old smiling eyes go deep into me. It had a hypnotic quality I found a bit eerie and it filled me with a quiet unease for some reason. I smiled back at him. He nodded, quietly laughed and then he nodded again. I took it as a sort of invitation, that he wanted to meet me. I caught myself up and chided myself that I was being presumptuous, doing the typical touristy thing. I felt that I was being a bit arrogant, a bit patronizing. After all, there was no reason why he would want to acquaint himself with an Australian tourist. It would be the height of bad manners to give him some money and even if I wanted to, it was a problem as to how much would be an acceptable amount that would not be insulting the old sirangi player. He had a dignity it was beholden of me to respect. Thinking it over I began turning away to see what Milly wanted me to see. It was my retreat. A shop was displaying several brightly colored beautiful silk scarves, all so exotic and subtle. I knew they were of the kind that Milly loved and for which she was always on the look out. I heard what turned out to be more than a cackle. It was a laugh. His laughter was a dry cackle. He stopped playing and looked up to address us.

"Hullo uncle. How are you?" he asked.

It was often a feature of Asian greeting for certain elderly foreigners. I believe it was a hangover from a colonial past. But why "uncle"? It was a throw back to the imperial period of the Raj, I thought.

We were both surprised and pleased he chose to speak to us.

"Thank you. We are fine," I replied. "How are you?"

"I am an old man. Sometimes up. Sometimes down," he replied, with a laugh.

"You come to Singapore to buy or have happy time?" he asked.

"Maybe a bit of both," Milly replied truthfully.

He nodded and scraped out a few more bars on his sirangi. The instrument absorbed him for the moment, I thought. Then he stopped playing and looked at us as if considering what his next move should be.

"You know what this is?" he asked holding out the stringed instrument.

"A sirangi," replied Milly, who recognized it from the times she had spent in rural India.

This pleased the old man. It brought a light into his eyes. I thought it cemented a certain bond between us. It was unusual knowledge coming from materialistic foreigners. That one such should have been somewhat familiar with something of the island culture he must have found gratifying. He smiled and nodded, but held out his right hand as if he would detain us.

"It is much more, my friend. This is the link to the world I knew as a child. It brings my childhood into this year, 2010. It is a time machine."

He chuckled.

He laughed the way an old man would. It was gentle and touched with a certain sadness at he passing of so much of a life time.

"My body feels like it is the body of an old man. Full of pain and disease."

He flexed his arthritic fingers to find a little relief.

"My heart feels like the heart of a child. Full of the music my mother and father brought into my life. You like it?"

We hastened to agree that we did. I felt I should try and tell him what it meant to me but I knew it meant as much for Milly whose childhood had been spent in rural Bihar where she and her family were the only Christians who lived there in the Raj years. The Indian connection was still very strong in her. It held only the merest tenuous hold on me, however. But I was still appreciative of this cultural icon. I felt the call of the past years in India. This was the music that transcended frontiers and diverse cultures.

The three of us fell silent with this quietly delivered comment. I felt the magic of his simple wisdom pass over me like a benediction. It made me feel suddenly humble. I wondered how this chance meeting with a Chinese minstrel in Singapore could bring us sharply and unexpectedly in touch with a part of our past. It was quite revealing how differently we both reacted. This was what we discussed over dinner later that night.

"Thank you for your time, sir," I said.

"Enjoy your life, friend. Never lose the child in your heart," he said slowly. "Listen to the music of your past life and clasp tightly the gems of wisdom of your inheritance."

Was there some insight that made him utter these strange and intriguing words? I stood looking at him in wonder at what had just transpired. Was it possible that our souls had been in some kind of intuitive communication; likeness calling to likeness? I was finding it difficult to cope with this explosion that had the energy of an epiphany. I was suddenly into denial; surely not. Why not? I argued back and forth in the few moments that enfolded us both.

He returned to his sirangi and played as if we weren't there any longer. Nor was he. He seemed to have passed into a trance, so deeply immersed was he in his music. This was nothing like the Singapore we thought we'd find. This was no longer the world of towering chrome and glass twenty first century ultra-modern urbanization, high finance, international trade of an encroaching new order that threatened it could swallow and silence the music of the sirangi player. But for now, the modernity was suddenly ever so far away and here was a history that lingered in all its fairy tale romance and yearning for the past. Momentarily we had been transported to a world we couldn't define but wasn't quite alien at the same time. We had it in each of us when we were children, unknown to each other, hundreds of miles apart but drawn together into this shared experience here in Sago Lane where the times, past and present intersected.

THE SONG OF MAD MARY

The fog had slipped in late at night and blanketed a weak July dawn. Grey swirling wraiths heavily laden with moisture seemed to rise and fall, and out of the bleak greyness came the raucous cries of ghostly gulls that swooped in and out of the fog as the birds flashed over the limestone native prison and disappeared again. Their cries brought a touch of sadness to the scene. They seemed to have an insight into the ways of human beings.

The crude and rugged roof thatched limestone building spewed out a thin column of smoke that lost itself in the thickening morning air. As yet no one had stirred out of the place. Night lights still emanated from barred, soulless windows that faced the sea that heaved itself upon the shore that was rocky almost all around the island, and then raced back out into the heaving motion from where they had come. The ocean was a brooding presence that swallowed up the human edifice in its immensity.

Out of the fog a fragile fishing vessel glided gradually into view and tied up alongside a crude jetty. Two long-coated figures slowly made their way up the stony path to Carnac House. The younger man was bare-headed. His damp mass of black hair spread wildly over his heavy brow. He scowled in a manner of one on a dark mission. The older man was stately, black-hatted and moved slowly and with some dignity. The younger man forged ahead and knocked on the door which was opened immediately. Their arrival had been watched from within as if they had been expected.

"Captain Irwin, sir. Please come in."

Captain Irwin stepped into Carnac House and removed his hat and great-coat which were whisked away by the obliging matron. He dusted off droplets of moisture and rubbed his hands together to improve his circulation. His breath left his body like twin jets. The room was briefly examined to familiarize himself with the interior and clearly he wasn't pleased.

"Good morning to you, Mrs Conroy and Lt Morgan. I trust you have been keeping well."

"Very well, thank you, sir," murmured both of them. Lt Morgan greeted the other perfunctorily. Lt Dawson followed them into the house as he blew warmth into his gloves. It took a little time for both visitors to get comfortable.

Three or four women, wives of prison waders, huddled inside a small adjacent room that in the background had a number of children who whispered furiously to each other, and stole sly, furtive looks at the backs of those who had just arrived. They were both inquisitive and curious. The eldest was a blond boy who ventured closest to the strangers and bade them a good morning. He was immediately hustled off by Mrs Conroy in a stern but motherly way.

Away from the presence of children they entered into a formal and business-like room that seemed to portend a gravity that needed secrecy and hard handling.

A gust of wind briefly rattled the canvas around the windows. The gloom of mid-July had found its way firmly into Carnac House. The inhabitants moved in mysterious shadows and the newly arrived emulated them. A gray-haired bespectacled man presently emerged from another room at which they had paused as they all whispered their greetings. They then got down to the nature of their business that had brought them to the island.

"She's no better, Capt Irwin, I regret to inform you, sir. She is in no pain, though. There's hardly any pulse, and there's been no fever," said old Dr Bryant, shaking his head in some confusion as if to disclaim any knowledge of what was bringing this strange condition on her. He anxiously searched the two faces as if begging to be believed.

"Has she lost consciousness?" asked Captain Irwin.

With head at a reflective angle Bryant took a little time to reply, and when he did it was with no certainty. A gentle cough began his reply.

"Strange that you should ask. Er- no, no, I would not say so although her eyes are closed in some sort of wakeful slumber."

Lt Dawson looked quickly at Irwin and saw a frown on the captain's face. Wakeful slumber? The gesture was not lost on Lt John Morgan whose duty it was to administer Carnac House and the penal block. He shuffled forward to the edge of the bed on which lay the strange woman who was known as Mary Ann Tagore to all. He cleared his throat.

"Ever since the prisoner was brought to Carnac House, sir, at your request, as you will no doubt recall, she has been in a strange sort of sleep. Not quite a sleep, if you follow me."

"Under her eye lids there seems to pass a sort of life that is reflected in her face. It's neither exactly troubled nor serene," interrupted the doctor, "but in a struggle to come to grips with something that seems deep rooted."

By now they had all arranged themselves around the bed and stared down at the strange, inert figure of a young woman. In the doorway Lt Morgan asked the hatchet-faced Mrs Conroy to brew up some tea for the visitors and break out some biscuits as well.

All eyes dwelt on the sleeping pale and gaunt sprite-like woman. Lt Dawson stepped closer and bent over her, peering into her face. He listened for her breathing and gently felt her pulse, shaking his head in some discomfiture.

"She's gone!"

At this everyone shuffled forward, consumed by curiosity and yet quite fearful.

"She's stopped breathing," whispered Dawson.

"No, no, Richard," said the doctor. "That's not so. That's how she breathes. She's been breathing like that since they brought her in a week ago. It's an unusual sort of controlled respiration. I'm told it is a sort of mysterious oriental contrivance. These people are known for these strange and outlandish practices and rituals. It is said that some have actually died and come back to life shortly after that. A sort of resurrection, perhaps? Strange, don't you think?" he added to no one in particular; more to himself than anyone.

By now another figure had pushed into the crowded space. John Connolly, courier, quietly joined the assembly. He had brought a message, but was temporarily distracted by what he was looking at. His pale face was awash in amazement, his brow furrowed. He wondered at what he was witnessing.

"That's part of her cultist practice, Captain Irwin, sir. She has spoken to me about a way of breathing and seeing she learnt in Bengal, India."

He spoke without a glance at any of the others, but steadfastly gazed at the face of Mary Ann Tagore whose face looked as if it were cast in marble.

"Connolly, what are you doing here? When did you get in?" inquired Irwin.

"Shortly before you, sir. I am to inform you that Mr Samson and the rest of his committee informs you, sir, that the meeting has been postponed. 'The Parmelia' hasn't got back from King George Sound as yet."

"Oh, all right, thank you," replied Irwin testily. "Can't be helped, I suppose."

He seemed too lost in thought to be irritated any further. His brows were tightly gathered. A deep and trembling breath escaped from him. He asked Connolly if she were alone and was informed that William Owen had helped him by rowing her in.

"Owen? Owen?" mumbled Irwin.

He had never liked the meddlesome school teacher. He was a bit of a nuisance about the colony. A silence brooded over the room and threatened to swell when they heard a low rumble. It came from the recumbent form of the woman.

Captain Irwin strained forward to catch what it was she was trying to say. Her lips trembled; she strained in the effort. Sweat creased her brow.

"...trail forks left as quarry... forest, thin...quarry face... looks like quarry face... quarter moon trapped in tree tops..." and then a silence fell from her lips. It was sung in a wailing sort of way that was both sweet and sad.

Just then Mrs Conroy arrived and whispered that tea and biscuits were served in the dining room. Dr Bryan lifted a hand to stop her from going on. Her interruption was a nuisance. He let his irritation be seen.

"...ridge runs along northern escarpment...forests become dense...native tracks...easterly direction...twelve men and three women..."

Lt Dawson whispered that recently some settlers had been reported moving up into that area without authorization. They had been warned that no protection would be offered if they disobeyed. But that had not stopped them, evidently.

"...monster...red in tooth and claw ..."

Her eyeballs moved under the thin covering membrane as she grimaced and fell silent, her breathing more perceptible. Her lips parted slowly. Dr Bryan quickly felt her forehead and shook his head.

"Ravens live in white hearts, Midgegooroo,
they tore yours out with lead,
maggots live in white hearts, Midgegooroo,
they'll feed upon you dead."

She sang the song in a falsetto.

Captain Irwin looked around, clearly bewildered and waited for someone to explain the song to him. A cloud must have passed across the sun just then as the light, or what there was of it, dimmed. The room fell silent. Then they heard her again.

"...red in tooth and claw..."

Irwin straightened up and moved away to the door, scratching his chin. He turned to face Lt Dawson.

"Any sighting of such wild animals?" he asked.

"No, sir, not as far as we have been able to ascertain. We have never come across anything like that. No carnivores in these parts, sir."

"She wasn't talking about wild animals," hissed Owens in contempt. "Only something worse." He sounded disgusted.

From across the rooms they could hear the children at play. They were getting louder. One of the lads, louder than any others, was heard to ask if Mad Mary was at it again. A woman hushed him up quickly.

"Is that what they are calling her, Mrs Conroy?" sharply, pointedly ignoring Owen's interjection of a while ago. "Mad Mary?"

"Children pick up grown ups' conversation, like as not, sir. I don't suppose they mean anything by it."

The Captain ignored her as he turned to attend to what Lt Dawson had started to say, as they headed to the dining room. "You may be disappointed to learn that only three Clydesdales and five stallions for the constabulary survived the crossing. We had to destroy the others unfortunately."

The Captain nodded grimly, shaking his head.

"I have let them know that we need more horses for the police here. Clydesdales are OK for the farms."

"Begging your pardon, Captain," said Dr Bryan after a few minutes silence, "there seems to be some confusion about her exact status. There has been some talk about her being indentured to the Lee Steere establishment."

"And there has been nothing from the Colonial Secretary's office."

"Even so, we know how in the colonies, de facto relationships establish themselves on a legal basis," came the reply.

All he got was a mumbled reply.

They adjourned for a tea and biscuits break. In that time they spoke about the social life in the Swan Valley and the outlying areas. There was at last better communication between Mandurah and Fremantle now that Peel had got his plans off the ground. They praised his initiatives.

Tea and biscuits having been done with the officers felt a little bit more relaxed. The morning advanced slowly to midday, brightening up a bit more to lift the spirits of those on Carnac. Lt Morgan came in from the stacked log piles with an arm full of fire wood to help the struggling fire to warm the room some more.

"What exactly do we know about this woman?" asked Dr Bryan.

The question came suddenly and caught everyone by surprise by its suddenness. No one ventured to oblige. All eyes turned to Captain Irwin who shrugged tiredly and hazarded a response.

"In the April of 1839 the 'Gaillardon' sailed into port. Mostly linen, wheat and hardware for the carpenters and Royal Engineers. Four paid passengers and half a dozen volunteers for the 63rd Foot."

He paused and wiped his face with a large handkerchief.

"Also Ezekiel Saunders with letters of introduction from the Governor of Bengal.."

"Any relation of John Saunders, sir?"

"Aye, son, some problem there, it's going to be. Aye. Sent here to do a stint in the Swan Valley settlement, or what there is of it."

"Poor devil," someone offered.

"Didn't last long, did he? Wasn't long before he got washed off the deck of the cutter whilst fishing off Rottnest. That left the young woman, Mary Ann Tagore on her own without his support and patronage, and no survival skills of her own," Irwin continued.

"To be a burden on the colony, I suppose, to be fed and looked after," said Mrs Conroy, with a supercilious sniff.

"Well, that's not the way it turned out. No one seems to know about the Saunders' estate. He was to have bought Dove Cottage on the hill outside Fremantle but Peel says no money changed hands. After his death the woman disappeared into native lands along with some settlers who have since returned sadly disillusioned. But without her. It appears from what they said that she disappeared into the wilderness. When she wandered into Fremantle later the Lee Steeres offered her an indenture. She learnt housekeeping and worked as a maid, but she worked half-heartedly at best. Lazy I suppose."

"And soon broke the terms of her indenture, turned to stealing and spent a month with some wild Irish baggage and ended up eventually in a Round House cell," put in Lt Morgan.

"A pity she was," said Dr Bryan. "I don't think she fitted in anywhere and I don't think she cared very much for the Lee Steeres. They were too much for her."

"A waste of time, if you ask me," said Mrs Conroy unrelentingly.

Owen coughed critically, trying to contain his anger and to catch their attention. He looked into their faces.

"That is unwarranted and uncharitable, I'll have you know, Mrs Conroy and anyone else who feels the same.." said Owen. "There's more to Mary Ann Tagore..."

"You mean Mad Mary, as she is known around here, sir," said Mrs Conroy pursing her lips.

"Mary Ann," went on Owen in the skirmishing, putting a telling stress on the name Mary Ann,"if you will, please, is very much maligned and misunderstood person. Her cultural background and refinements..."

"Refinements?" came with a whispered hiss. "Indian refinements, you mean!" she said.

"...did not equip her to settle in and no one helped the lonely woman, either. I have no doubt that she and Ezekiel Saunders would not have remained here much longer had he not died so tragically," concluded Owen softly.

By now a watery sun had struggled out as they trooped out into the weak sunlight. The mainland looked hazy. The "Duke of Bedford" a recent arrival from Sydney lazily bobbed about idly at anchor. Some boats with their loads of fishermen lay scattered across the bay. Gulls skimmed over the waves around them hoping for a show of generosity of playful fishermen, as had happened from time to time when little fishes were thrown overboard at them.

"Hmm-m, perhaps not. Perhaps they should never have come out to the Swan River Colony. We need men and women of sterner stuff. Hardly a place and time to indulge in – Bryan, what really happened at the Round House? It's still so confusing. Far too many felons incarcerated in such a small holding house. I hear that -"

Lt Dawson interrupted Captain Irwin with, "Forty six prisoners in six available cells, sir, one of which contains five women and sixteen natives in two other cells."

He tried to keep anger out of his voice. His words came out choked and in half whispers.

Captain Irwin looked at him longer than what may have been necessary.

He turned back to Carnac House and the others trooped along behind him.

"They brought the Tagore woman straight there from the magistrate's court. I believe there's some records of the proceedings. I haven't had the opportunity to call across to read them. But I will, to be sure. She was hustled in and issued a blanket. Father Kelly brought her some clean clothes. Those Irish whores seemed enthralled by her. She spoke to them honestly and earnestly. When she wasn't singing strange songs she'd sit for hours her eyes closed and swaying and hardly breathing," said William Owen.

"I hear the native prisoners were very interested in her," said Lt Morgan.

"Yes. Quite so. She was very curious about the lot of them, especially Midgegooroo's son, Tulicatwallee, who we brought over from King George Sound last year. It's only the warders she couldn't abide. She would scream at them from time to time calling them murderers. They would have cheerfully killed her if they could," said Owen.

Lt Morgan and Mrs Conroy led them into a bigger and better-aired room that had a large table in the centre on which were tea and sandwiches. They had managed to serve up a salad and some sort of sausages and potato mash. A whisper of satisfaction and thanks went around the room.

The branches of a nearby banksia danced strenuously. Beyond, waist high above the bushes, could be seen the figures of three elderly native prisoners under escort making their way down from the Carnac holding centre to the shore, but that wasn't what caught Lt Morgan's attention. He called out the news that a long boat was rowing ashore.

"By the way, Dawson, wasn't it you who brought her in?" asked Captain Irwin, helping himself to some salad and sausages, ignoring anything that threatened to disrupt his meal.

"Yes, sir, I was given a detail from the 63rd. We tracked her to a head stream of the Swan River where she loved to visit. Talk about the Noble Savage! Jean Jacques Rousseau would have loved her. She luxuriated in her forest world. Seemed to caress the trunks of the trees and fondle the branches and leaves. Quite daft."

Morgan laughed and suggested that what she really needed was a man. Mrs Conroy was of the view that no man would be quite so daft to have anything to do with her. The interruption was brief. Dawson looked at them with raised eyebrows and an obvious disdain and then continued.

"She didn't resist capture. Came along as meek as a lamb. We got her to the Lee Steere family but she refused to stay despite their show of goodwill and acceptance. They are such generous people and good Christian souls. We had been followed all the way by a party of natives who were clearly hostile and took careful watching but they stopped at the river. I've seen two or three of them since loafing about the place as they like to do. Bold as brass."

Owen had gone out briefly and returned with his head slightly wet by a passing shower.

"Colonel Henderson and Lt Wray on their way in, Captain Irwin, sir," he said, shaking the water off himself. He spoke solemnly as if bringing ominous news. Irwin nodded his thanks. While the assembled company waited their entry, white-faced and trembling Mrs Conroy sidled up to Dr Bryan and urgently whispered something to him whereupon he hurriedly left the room which by now was filled with wisps of wood fire smoke. The others courteously advanced to welcome the newly arrived. Colonel Henderson and Lt Wray stiffly and formally returned the greetings.

"Ah, Captain, good to meet up with you again. How is the work on the new bridge coming along? You're with the Royal Engineers for the present, are you not? Is that correct?"

"Yes, sir. Quite correct. We also have some lads from the 63rd on the job as well. Too much slackness settling in, I'm afraid, but measures to deal with that are in hand, I assure you," replied Captain Irwin.

"Good. Good. I am sure they are. And you'll be needing another cell block here on Carnac I am informed. It will come soon enough, you can be quite sure," said Colonel Henderson who moved imperiously deeper into the rooms. He took off his gloves, moving close to the fireplace. Soon they were more relaxed as they had tea and biscuits. Then the conversation became business-like again.

"As you know the "Bedford" is now in port. Came in from Botany Bay en route to Southampton. I had the pleasure of calling on Lord Ellesmere who is returning to England." The relief in his voice suggested it wasn't too soon, either. He sniffed with satisfaction at the prospect.

"You will be happy to know that he inquired about one Mary Ann Tagore, daughter of a famous Indian barrister and intellectual and poet of sorts, Dwarkanath Tagore, who enjoys regal patronage, as you might be aware. He has some very powerful connections. Unfortunately, she stubbornly followed that scallywag Saunders out to the blasted Swan River Colony here. Sad business all round, wouldn't you say? But then I am sure you would have taken good care of her. How is she? You must arrange a meeting with her for me."

A terrible silence of ponderous dread fell upon the assembled officers of Carnac House. They went white wondering where Dr Bryan was and what he was doing instead of being here to answer the coming questions.

"The real reason for my visit here is to let Morgan and Conroy know that they are to prepare Miss Tagore for a visit to Lord Ellesmere tomorrow. I expected them to be present here to receive me. This is most unsatisfactory, you know. His lordship wishes to entertain her and have a talk with her, as you would expect. He wants to offer her his personal escort into Southhampton. It is well known that he has assumed personal care and sponsorship for her. This would register very favorably with the Admiralty, as you would expect. We here would be only too glad to get her off our hands and be well rid of our responsibility. The colony does not need women like her. Can't see her as a good seed carrier."

He paced the floor restlessly looking out of the door one moment and the window the next. He smiled to see children racing off down the grassy slope to the jetty all excited. His smile slowly dissolved into a taught frown in sudden misgiving about something. Then Mrs Conroy and Dr Bryan entered the room quietly like a couple of ghosts. All eyes turned to them. Mrs Conroy looked away, fiddling with her apron awkwardly. She resolutely avoided looking into the eyes of any one in the room. Instead, she played nervously wit her house keys.

"Yes?" asked Colonel Henderson.

There was no reply. Dr Bryan stared away past Colonel Henderson to nowhere in particular as he dreaded having to face everyone. The voices of the children at play drifted up to them. They had come racing back from the jetty in wild pursuit. Pursuit of another kind was reaching its climax in Carnac House.

"Mary Ann Tagore is dead," announced Dr Bryan.

There was a sharp intake of breath all round.. More than a statement of fact, the announcement sounded like the report of an execution.

"What!" exploded Stirling, his face red with anger and surprise.

"Damn it all, how is it you people could not keep a better scrutiny over her. By God, there's going to be hell let loose on some of you. Dereliction of duty and responsibility, I say."

They all made an energetic entry into the room where Mary Ann Tagore lay dead. Her eyes blankly stared up at the ceiling. They seemed to be blessed with a look of release. They were past revealing fear or anger.

Some stared at the end of their careers. Some began making out excuses that would have to be proffered to Lord Ellesmere.

"My God, what are we going to do?" asked Mrs Conroy heavily.

"I really do not know and frankly, my dear, I don't care," said Dr Bryan. "I hope to buy a passage back home on the Bedford. As for you lot," he said, staring at Governor Stirling in particular, "can rot in the Swan River Colony or in hell."

THE WINTER OF THE HUMAN HEART

Father O'Brien had just returned where he had fruitlessly searched for his missal. Age was debilitating his memory. It wasn't the first time he had misplaced his missal. The greyness, damp and the cold of winter wasn't any help, either. Somehow it would turn up somewhere as it usually did. Saint Anthony had not let him down ever. He chose to forget the times Tony was no help. Why spoil a great story. This didn't worry him unduly but it was becoming a bit of a nuisance. He opened the microwave where he found a casserole dear Mrs Charlton had left for him. He busied himself setting the table and getting out his favorite bottle of Cabernet Shiraz he loved to drink this time of the day.

He sat down and opened the day's newspaper and read the headlines to see if any stories caught his attention. Half way through his meal he saw a silver Mercedes pull up with a rich whisper that just about reached him. It was John Clarke who had come about some of the church's financial dealings he supposed. He felt just a bit uneasy as he usually felt somehow before something disturbing landed on his doorstep..

"Come in, John, the door is open," he called out.

"I can come back later if you wish, Father. I will let you finish your lunch first. What I have come about won't take long."

They spoke briefly about local matters and the church's social life. They could have gone on a while longer but John

Clarke became eager to get to the point, and it wasn't going to be easy. He wondered if he was really stalling.

"Have some wine, John," invited the priest. "Youv'e eaten, I'm sure."

"Yes, thank you, I have, but a little wine won't go astray."

He sipped the red appreciatively and held up the bottle to find out a little more about it. It was good stuff. He sat back and made himself more comfortable.

"Well? What's the matter, now? Tell me," invited the priest, putting down his knife and fork and turned a smiling face to his guest.

Clarke drew his chair forward and considered how to handle the subject. He cleared his throat and looked into the priest's eyes.

"Yes?" asked the priest entreatingly as he wished to get to him and help him.

"Well, father, it is something that has been worrying me more than a bit, I have to say. Before I say any more it is understood that all of it is to be highly confidential, naturally."

"Naturally," replied the priest, suspecting something deep.

"Not even to my wife. Especially not to her."

The priest's brow clouded for a moment as a troubled light came into his eyes. He didn't see this coming.

"This is a most unusual request coming from a man who has both a virtue for his frankness and openness and is known to be very caring and devoted to Maria, his beloved wife," said the troubled priest. "I will do all I can to be of help to both of you who are my dear friends more than merely wonderful examples of good people to the community."

"It's the Rwandan refugee, Pius Lubanga. He's been hanging around the front yard too many times with nothing to do but moon about the place and looking at the place expecting something or someone. I'm beginning to feel it has been a big mistake getting so close to him to make him feel safe and respected to compensate for his traumatic life in Rawanda. It has unsettled Maria who is beginning to have nightmares about him and the way our little girl, Camilla, adores him. And he adores her. That worries us the most. I suppose it is all in innocence finding a natural expression in their feelings for each other." An uneasy silence settled in. John Clarke's entwined fingers turned and twisted as he nervously searched Father O'Brien's face for some hope.

"Yes? Well, I'm waiting for the problem, John," said the priest.

John Clarke then tried shifting the focus from off himself.

"It's Maria whom I am really worried about, Father."

"Has he said or done anything reprehensible? Worse still, has he interfered with Camilla that we should worry about? As you and the whole congregation are well aware of, I personally am mentoring Pius who is a really good Catholic man who deserves more love and protection than anyone in our community..as you well know. I find him to be an exceptionally good soul, very hard-working, honest and devout. But, if he's done anything bad...you know...I want to know now so that I can call him in and give him a talking to."

Father O'Brien's voice quavered and began breaking up.

"Not directly, sort of...but for over a week he has been crawling into the doll house I made for Camilla at the back of the garden. Little Camilla has been taking food out to him...playing at cooking up meals which he has been eating," replied Clarke.

"What a lovely thought and what a display of idealized innocence, the way it should be. We should take that as an example set for all of us, John, But where's the problem?"

It didn't turn out to be such a short visit for which Clarke had hoped earlier. He poured out his heart to the priest hoping for something more than understanding and sympathy. He didn't get anything like that. Father O'Brien implored him not to call in the police as Clarke had hinted at because it wasn't really a serious matter the father thought. It was sure to exacerbate matters in the parish where he was well aware that many viewed Pius Lubanga and his three other Rwandan fellow refugees with ill-concealed suspicion and distaste. It was a sad fact that Australian Catholics were ambivalent about their attitude to the refugees or asylum seekers. The Rwandans had entered the country legally having been screened and approved by the UNHRC. Hutus had been welcomed by the Catholic Commission for resettlement of displaced persons.

These were like no other Africans now living in the country. They were taller and much more darker skinned than most with coarse and thick skin and strange yellow eyes you see in most people suffering from jaundice. Unfortunately they exuded a strange reptilian image. Most Australians found difficulty in getting close and befriending them. Language was another major problem. Apart from the frugal nature of the hospitality they received they felt the Australian cold more than other refugees. Sometimes the temperature dropped to below freezing point. Then they felt homesick as they missed the hot and humid forests and the savannah.

The days passed slowly. It rained and rained. Streets became like swollen streams. Playgrounds became inland seas. When the rains ceased the temperatures again plummeted. The land soon became overrun with weeds. Pius came faithfully every day to weed the garden and surrounding areas of the house and remove the storm detritus fallen around the house. He found time to enjoy the doll house that Clarke had built for his daughter. It must be said that Camilla both cajoled and ordered him to join her in the cubby. She even secreted out a blanket and pillow without anyone noticing. It came as a shock to Maria when she found out what had been going on.

It did no good talking to John about it. He would only take the matter to Father O'Brien who had the cheek to come and lecture her about Catholic charity and forbearance. That made her angry. She decided to be direct and talk to Camilla about the matter. It didn't help when a secret guilt grew in her. Would that result in poisoning the little mind against Africans in the community? That wouldn't be fair. She adored her little girl and wanted to protect her.

When the signs of winter became spring, people's minds and hearts thawed and opened. But winter sometimes remained in people's hearts. The winter of the human heart was harder to thaw and let in the growing warmth all around. One day John Clarke came home to hear that the police had called. They had found the body of Pius Lubanga in a garbage dump not far from the city. He had been poisoned. They dreaded breaking the news to Camilla. It was going to be a huge problem, they knew. She came in from chasing butterflies and the news that Pius hadn't turned up for some reason. When the news of his death was finally and clumsily broken at last Camilla's face went white, tears flowed down her cheeks and her bottom lip quivered. She fled outside and howled her loss to the world outside. It took a long time to quieten her and console her. Maria held her tightly to her self. They would have to be very watchful over her in the days to come. Camilla refused food and withdrew into her inner world of silence. Her doll house became her refuge where neither her parents nor her friends were welcome.

Spring brought the house mice to life again. They had to be dealt with decisively or they would breed out of control as they once did a few years ago. John called out from the rose bed where he had done some weeding.

"Maria," he called out. There was no response. He tried again but still there was no response. Strange. Then from within he thought he heard a stifled response. He went inside to the laundry.

"Maria," he said, "Have you seen the Ratzack anywhere? Where do we keep it?"

Her inert body didn't move. He found her slumped over the washing machine, head down.

"Maria?" he whispered as he raised her tear-streamed face to his. He kissed her tears. "What's the matter, dear?"

Outside Camilla sang a doleful song as she plucked flowering weeds from the garden. Something Pius would have done had he been with her still.

Slowly she withdrew the Ratzac from where she had hidden it behind some soiled linen which were ready for washing. John with trembling hand took the poison and stared at it in disbelief. All he could stammer was "How?..."

"I found it with her toy house cooking utensils she uses to cook scraps of meals for herself. She had left all the utensils for me to clean I suppose. It was only an act of providence that she didn't eat it also. She must have left it for him, poor thing," said Maria.

Poor thing? John was lost in thought. Poor thing?

WHEN THE GOD OF DEATH
IS THE DEATH OF GOD

Haiti is the poorest country in the West Indies. It shares an island with the Dominican Republic to its east. Poverty hasn't in past times prevented the people's fervent adherence to their God. They loved to demonstrate their devotion in song and dance to show their love of God. They have very colorful Creole and musical expressions of faith, full of fervour and religious passion. They were fully supported in this by the Roman Catholic church which had taken hold of and absorbed these overt demonstrations of religious fervor into a cultural identity which strengthened the Church.

On Tuesday, the 12th of January, 2010, the working day was almost at an end. Some workers were beginning to make their way home, looking forward to relaxing and a good night meal, looking forward to a time to relax with loved ones in a happy family life. It was such a peaceful day under a fleecy sky where indolent clouds hovered about lazily. Love embraced man and nature.

The serenity wasn't to last long. At 16:53 precisely Haiti jumped about 10cm into the air with an ear-splitting roar. An earthquake of magnitude 7:00 hit Haiti. Rows of palm trees and all the modest buildings along the beach outside the coastal town of Leogane 25 km west from the capital, Port au Prince, came crashing down and the sea leapt in and with the massive quakes destroyed the town completely. Fishing vessels were washed up more than 100 metres into the town. It looked like a gigantic angry hands had spitefully uprooted all signs natural and human habitation. That wasn't the worst thing that happened.

It was a very black day when the heart of Haiti was torn apart. The two major spiritual centers, the Anglican Cathedral of the Holy Trinity and the Roman Catholic Cathedral of Our Lady of Assumptions disappeared in a cloud of rubble and accompanying choking dust into which both disappeared only to re-appear shortly in heaps of heartbreaking debris and broken prayers. Shattered masonry, a tangle of wrought iron, exposed brickwork and wooden ribs of heavy timber reached up clawing at the heartless sky above.

Broken bodies of angels, an assortment of saints, and Jesus and Mary could be seen lying about desecrated altars. Michael the Arch Angel had been decapitated. His severed head still wore a smile despite all the destruction it had suffered. And despite their own broken bodies and other personal losses, men, women and children, maimed, bloodied and covered in dust and grime ran frantically, wild-eyed, screaming, and tried to salvage whatever they thought should be salvaged. Some dropped dead as a consequence of their very brave but fruitless efforts. Amongst the dead was the much-loved Archbishop Joseph Serge Miot. The irate God did not discriminate. He took the rich and powerful and the common, the pious and the sinners, the richest and poorest alike. What was he angry about? No one really knew. Prayers would still ascend for him to forgive them and relent his vengeance on whatever wrong living of which they had been guilty.

It must have been mostly the poor he didn't much care for, it seemed. The slum city of Cite Soleil was no more. Most of the 300,000 who perished were the poorest of this slum, as if there wasn't enough of a tragedy whilst they lived their poverty stricken lives. Bodies lay all over the place in various and bizarre poses of their mortality. The stench of death made the capital city stink like a slaughter house. Rotting corpses littered the city. Lean, uncared for dogs roamed the ruins and knew where the corpses were.

What clutched at the heart most was the sight of school children who died in play. Skipping ropes still in the hands of a few. Their innocence abused by the coldness of their brutal death. Flying sheets of glass had decapitated three who were nearest shops. The heads had rolled some distance away driven by the impetus of tremors. The eyes and mouth of each head was a hideous grimace. These children were found in the Cite Soleil. There would probably be none to mourn them. Their parents lay dead in their homes or where they worked. That day over 300,000 died horribly. There was to be a mass burial organized by the churches, a further indignity added to the tragedy, but it was inevitable that it was the only response possible to death of such a magnitude. Dogs were the only ones who seemed to come out on top. Some were seen eating the choicest sections they could tear off the corpses. Men who had enough energy swore as loudly as they could and threw stones at them that scared them off. Other dogs were seen dragging off remains of the dead to some secret locations where they could eat in peace and be safe from having their meal disturbed.

Even whilst the survivors and the army and police and paramedics organized some semblance of cleaning up, getting rid of rubble, restoring order and pulling the dead and wounded out of wrecked buildings, the ground kept trembling, shock after shock, bringing down those parts of buildings that managed to hang on precariously to their parent structures. Rescuers had to keep dodging falling debris. Men lost their balance whilst others performed balancing feats never seen before as they tried to keep vertical. There could be heard cries of caution and desperate warnings ringing through Haiti's hell on earth, as the work proceeded valiantly in the shattered capital of Port au Prince. Volunteers wore masks or bandanas over their faces or they couldn't have worked in the ubiquitous stink of rotting corpses.

Many were seen vomiting and coughing. The dust that carried the stench also half-choked them.

Ambulances, sirens screaming, ran futile missions crazily jumping up and down as they negotiated one pile of loose rubble from another, always in danger of capsizing. Survivors anxious to secure their help for severely wounded loved ones ran alongside screaming profanities and beating the sides of the ambulances whilst screeching for help till they were left in the wake of the racing vehicles. Some noticed the incongruous sight of a lonely cyclist above all things strangely making his way, swaying about the place trying to keep his balance all the while crying to the world, "Water. Please, give me water. My child is dying!"

The second day after the carnage, at the cemetery, facing the graves, a dais had been erected with what passed for an altar of sorts. Grieving parishioners brought their ravaged souls, broken bodies and tears, dressed in flowers and crosses. The diminutive and almost emaciated figure of the presiding priest, a Father Henri Rousseau, came to the steps he climbed with difficulty. He stood silently. Not seconds, but many minutes passed and those who came for solace and explanation asked why they had been so sorely punished.

They were looking for answers. Father Rousseau knew that and he had none to offer. He stared about him feeling incapacitated. He desperately sought words to explain the ordeal in such a way that their faith still lingered however sorely tested. "You, oh God, are our death, our strength and our Saviour" and here he choked and coughed. He spat out dust and bitterness. His lean body quivered. He was disheveled and all the worse for wear and looked exhausted as he might well have been. All the while tremors would run through the assembly and the timid amongst them would cry out and cling desperately to anyone nearest to them, but no one left.

"Why, oh God, why?" asked Father Rousseau.

His eyes covered the length and breadth of the crowded faithful who needed comfort and strength. He recognized the faces of all those who worshipped in the church regularly and regularly offered up good works for the poor and afflicted; he recognized in their faces the torment he himself felt and could not deny.

His hands extended, palms upturned, his gaze moved from left to right and still the silence ran into their mystery. The silence was the silence of the dead. It lasted a long time.

It seemed for ever. Faces looked painfully and angrily into the lonely and hurting figure of the priest. The mystery grew, palpable and unnerving. Then his voice spilt out into the chaos and pain with an effort. It was at first cracked and little more than a stutter, and afflicted with a sort of guilt at what he planned to say. In between his words they heard the cries that he refused to hold back. The hands that he held out to his flock trembled.

"You have heard it said from the altar of what was our Cathedral, you have heard it said from the days you were first able to speak and understand that our God is a God of love and justice, our defender and source of comfort and strength."

He stopped. His hand cupped his face and he gazed out at all who stood there before him. He wanted to cry out to them, "Why, oh why, do you flock to me at such a time as this? I hurt more than you. What do you want of me? What do you demand of your God?"

His eyes blazing he clenched his right fist and punched the air. He became the angry prophet of the Pentateuch. His hair was wild and unkempt, streaming in the wind that had now picked up around the scene of destruction and death.

"The Old Testament has its Yahweh, it's God of death and punishment. For us today, the God of Death is the Death of God. This God is powerless and reflects our own powerlessness. You cannot lift your hands to God for help; use them instead for burying your dead and rebuilding the Cathedral where a new faith must be born. Go to your homes and start to rebuild them for your families. Go to the broken homes of your neighbours and rebuild the community. Make the orphans your own children. Feed those who no longer have any food. Open your broken homes to those who have no homes. When you repair your homes help them to build theirs.

Today we must search for new answers. Asia has its Killing Fields of Cambodia. Europe has its Holocaust. In the Americas we today have our Haiti, our Port au Prince. In your spiritual journey you are at a crossroads and you have a choice to make. It must be made without anger. It must rebuild a meaningful community of human beings answerable to each other. When we bury our dead let us bury that anger. The new road, if there is to be a new road, must not be polluted with anger. Let your pain bless the way ahead. It is where you must turn. We will need new directions, a new vision, a new heaven and a new God."

His eyes blazed with an evolutionary ardor. His pain could not be contained. His clerical discipline was fully compromised. His parishioners stared with disbelief at his ranting. Some of the bolder ones nodded their support, but tentatively and almost fearfully but with fateful acceptance. Truth sometimes can be aborted; sometimes it has a dangerous birth. The consequence of the earthquake had an earth-shaking consequence at Port-au-Prince that day. Even as Father Rousseau spoke the quakes shifted the earth around them all and behind him masonry from the great cathedral kept falling off with an on-going rumble but soon no one looked around with alarm. Fear seemed to have been excised from their stupefied lives which were now too numbed with grief.

Long afterwards the after shocks seemed to have a life of their own. The earth still shook but slightly, the tremors not too eager to leave. The tremors on earth ran tremors in a distant heaven. The light that poured out of the parted clouds was the light from a new heaven.

THAT'S WHEN
THE SINGING STOPPED

The battle for Al Hamzi, 73 kilometers south west of Homs, had swung back and forth many times without a definitive result. Very little was left of the buildings; very few remained alive. Those who survived were either wounded or in a state of mental collapse and exhaustion. If you were to look for a hell on earth you would need to look no further. Here was one of thousand others.

The shelling had ended three days ago. Cautiously what was left of the ragged and exhausted population crept out to try and find some food and water. They foraged, bleeding, limping on crutches and cowering in fear, among the detritus of shattered homes hopeful of finding something to eat and water to drink. Most of what they picked up and sniffed they threw away in disgust. Some times they greedily quarreled about what they managed to find, scraps of food abandoned by some other hungry souls who had no time to eat or had to survive in panic. Survival comes in many ways. No children were to be seen anywhere. Lean, cadaverous-looking dogs wandered the streets. A lonely mangy cat was seen sniffing at something at a street corner. It pawed it tentatively, turned it over sneezed and then ran away into a darkened street.

At the end of the cobbled street stood the ruins of a one thousand year old Coptic church. Nearby was what once had been a playground for children. It had recently become pock-marked due to the shelling. Here hell played desperate and inhuman games of its own. So now it had been transformed into a wasteland. The trees around it had been knocked down and lay on their sides dying and withered, as was an old crone who had somehow come to share a refuge in the shattered bowels of what had been a building of sorts with three other much younger women. It was all part of the mystery of death and dying. How they came to be there sharing the shelter was another of the many mysteries of this war..They were all too afraid to venture out. That fear also made them wary and suspicious of each other. That was how the instinct of survival worked.

The younger women clearly shared no intimacy or sympathy for the crone whom they regarded with suspicion and hostility and robbed them of much of what was left of their humanity. Whatever the women said to each other was conveyed in conspiratorial whispers and sneers. They kept on glaring at the crone who disregarded their looks and whispers but continued with her tuneless singing which was more like a sort of chanting. Her old, sick and yellowing eyes darted this way and that but not seeing much more than a world no more than a few metres away. Those eyes were blurring and not able to make much of her world that was slowly breaking up around her.

Every now and then a shell exploded near by and the women cringed and shivered. The eldest in the group clung all the more tightly to the thin black cotton shawl she had wrapped tight around her bony frame that slithered about from one angle to another to get more comfortable and protected at the same time. Her black eyes darted about the ruins around her. She hissed something to the two others. Clearly she was a person of some authority. The youngest, a blonde teenager, had a dirty, bloodied bandage around her head. She couldn't take her hands away from her ears which she cupped to protect her from the sounds that traumatized her. Her eyes darted from left to right fearfully as she kept sobbing.

In between shell bursts came the sound of running feet and men's voices babbling in confusion. Commands were shouted and the running about began again as orders were carried out. Then an uneasy silence would develop for a while. Now the sound of booted footsteps at a trot approached the refuge. The women shuddered with fear that the sound of their breathing would betray their presence. The crone observed all this but didn't let it interrupt her tuneless singing which fell away and was barely audible at the time. The three others didn't know how to get rid of her, even though she had been the first to find the refuge. They didn't try to shut her up because they feared her for some reason. It may have been because of some superstitious dread that emanated from her. Their eyes never left her.

After a while her partly yellow and red bloodshot eyes closed with a click. She was transported away to another time and another place to which her singing took her. She saw the low-roofed house where she and her husband had lived and reared their ten children. They had lived in a friendly suburb with the local mosque just across the road from them. They were well-known to the friendly imam. It was from here her children and later, grand-children had grown up and gone out into the world and made successful lives of their own. The crone managed to cackle with what must have passed for a proud laugh. This made the other three fugitives clutch at each other more tightly and fearfully. There was no knowing where all the old woman's relatives now lived. Hopefully far from this hell of war. Her husband was long since dead, having left her the hut, a cow, a dog and a cat, and the many children to feed, clothe and bring up by herself. And she had done a good job till the war came and drove everyone away if it didn't killed them first. She had no idea where they had scattered and who now looked after them. Every day she mourned her many losses. She felt no one worried after her, an old hag for whom no one wanted to be responsible. She had too many needs.

Her thoughts were suddenly interrupted. Some trucks groaned up the road and pulled up outside their shelter. Commands were barked and other voices were raised in response. This went on for nearly an hour after which the trucks coughed into decrepit life and with difficulty lurched forward again. The silence that filled the void was not a very comforting one, rather was it a period of high anxiety during which the four women lived out their private hells.

The fourth, the old crone, would not have known what world she was in anyway. She had gone past knowing about all that. All she now did in between singing her cracked, endless song was to spit and then resume singing which would rise and fall in cadences and the three women would pause their whisperings and glare malevolently at her and wonder what to do about it. They once thought of driving her out but the eldest cautioned against it as this would draw the attention of lurking soldiers to them and then disaster would certainly follow the discovery. They had to put up with the old witch.

...there was once a little boy, who had only recently learned to run... loved to chase slow-moving footballs that were kicked for his benefit... he loved kicking the ball about. Maybe he would grow up to be a famous footballer and earn lots of money for his family. It was fun watching the little black dog, Prince, beat him to the ball and run about with it, the little boy chortling and chasing both of them... those were such happy days, she reminisced, wiping away her tears.

A long drawn out silence descended on the ruins of what was once a rural market town. In the silence could be heard vague sounds of movements from far and near. There was the occasional crump of overhead artillery followed by distant explosions. It appeared as if the fighting had shifted a little further away. Nothing clearly discernible but menacing all the same. Now and then these vague sounds would transform into the sounds of people in pain, calling out for water, for help, for some attention to ease their agonies. Then the silence would return. Again would come the cries for help and water. People suffering dreadful wounds cried out in pain. It sometimes sounded like the howling of animals. There was no one to rescue them, no one to ease their pain or no one to help them to die. This was a world where no one cared any more. Overhead a pitiless sun burned through a blue sky a heat that threatened to engulf everything.

The approach of a mechanical monster began to swell louder and louder. It churned up the earth as it went over the streets. The clanging of its mechanical parts came nearer and nearer. From its turret a long barrel of a canon bobbed up and down swinging about left to right, then right to left searching the territory ahead the way it swung in threatening arcs. A human head suddenly popped up from the inside and shouted something down into the bowels of the monster. Anything in its path, masonry, timber or glass shattered as the monster rolled inexorably over them, and worse, spewed out shredded human parts of anyone fallen in its part, wounded or dead. Running slowly along with it were soldiers with rifles at the ready, all of them trigger-happy. Every now and then someone would fire a burst at some imagined enemy, although no one had remained to oppose them. Many of the infantry were barely men. They should have been in school or at university instead of contributing their share of the bloody carnage. They picked their way amongst the corpses of those who had not retreated fast enough to new positions. If any wounded that may have remained even twitched they were immediately shot dead.

The boy soldiers laughed and sang as they went from one ruined building to another to make sure no enemy remained hidden. This was better than school or sitting in some dry as dust university lecture. They loved this adrenaline-charged life, taking risks and living with death. They had developed a blood lust. They were real men. They could do as they pleased, even kill if they had to. They developed delight in putting enemy soldiers to death. It made them swell with pride when they thought they were to be feared.

....tired eyes looked into the distance... saw a little one who was born with polio blowing bubbles... and trying to run on her deformed little feet... heard the sound of her laughter and her song picked up in cadence at the vision. This little grand-daughter was her favorite. She lived for her happiness...a slow smile played briefly on her cracked lips... eyes flickered and blinked as she tried to hang on to this sacred image and hold it before her. She needed to as she smelt fear near at hand. It helped to keep her courage up. The crone sang of her love for the little girl.

Ten uniformed men appeared momentarily at the hole in the building that housed the four women. They chatted loudly as they called to one another. They looted anything that took their fancy. They poked about the ruins. An officer peered down from above the hole. He was more perceptive than the enlisted men. He caught sight of the refugees.

"Well, well, look here! What have we found in the shadows!"

He laughed at the spectacle and in anticipation of what they were going to do to them. The men also laughed as much to share their officer's elation as to establish a closer camaraderie. They were all brothers in arms and trying so hard to be hardened and experienced soldiers and to be seen as such by the officer. Besides, to the victors go the spoils.

They pounced on the younger women who knew their fate instantly but nevertheless put up a struggle as best they could. They kicked and bit as many as they were able to. They screamed for help and also let out a torrent of vitriolic abuse that made the soldiers burst out laughing. They retaliated with their rifle buts and boots.

"High-spirited women, eh! I like it that way. Bring me the youngest, that blonde," the officer demanded.

They dragged the three women away with them. In the distance the voices of the women being ravaged could still be heard. It was no different with these three women as it had been with all women who had had the misfortune of being found in this hellish theatre of pain and death and what was even worse than pain or death.

Back in the shelter a couple of minutes passed in the increased emptiness till a rat-face appeared again in the hole and peered down into the shelter as if he had forgotten something. An acne-pitted blond youth looked about like a ferret. He was on his way out but suddenly paused at the strange low-keyed singing of a very old crone. He shot her through her head. Blood spurted everywhere and her yellow eyes rolled over shut. Her cracked lips remained open. The singing ended; the world had lost its singer.

A Canticle For Calyute
or
The Last Warrior Chief

February was an unusual summer month in the year 1834. Every second or third day it had rained,sometimes quite heavily. From information handed down later, historians were able to say that a strong depression had moved over the land and only slowly moved away down south. The rains came on the back of the storm which had lashed the countryside the day before. The powerful winds had torn some saplings out of the earth and wrenched branches from trees. The Murray River was the graveyard of many such branches. All that had passed away for now and had left only a tired rain that served to remind people of the traumas of the recent days. However,on the last days of October it was very gray and cloudy and a steady, heavy drizzle kept falling. Along the banks of paper bark trees, and fern-lined river a group of thirty seven armed settlers had come to a halt.

Few were ordinary citizens, some half a dozen were settlement police, and fifteen others were drawn from the 21st Regiment regulars in their regimental red and black,and the others from Mounted Volunteer Force. The force had been assembled under Captain Stirling who had a growing reputation for ruthlessly putting down native lawlessness that usually ended in retaliations like theft accompanied with violence. This lawlessness morphed eventually into something political such as Calyute, the leader of the indigenous people of this part of the country. He let it be known that nothing short of expelling the invaders would satisfy the native people of the Swan Valley. He had already suffered under Irwin and Stirling. His wife,Yornup, had had her lower left leg shot away and they had shot and killed his son, Unia. He hated the usurpers and took every opportunity to destroy their property and steal whatever he could lay hands on as part payment for their presence on their lands.

Ellis,the richest settler who owned a number of buildings and tents in and near Mandurah, rode up to Captain Irwin and Governor Stirling. He had to restrain a fidgety horse under him as he spoke, "I don't like this silence,Governor Stirling. They are up to something,sir."

All he got was a "Hmm. What do you think about the problem ahead of us,Irwin?" he said turning to his personal assistant in a way that suggested only military men would know how and when to act. Ellis scowled at the affront and pulled his mount away to one side.

The men looked about them. Norcott,fondling his shotgun all the while, peered intently into every shrub and willow tree clumps as he searched for signs of movement along the banks. Branches broken off in the latest storm floated across the River Murray in places. Its movements in the water made the settlers and soldiers all the more jittery as they jumped at the prospect of camouflaged indigent warriors floating towards them. He was visibly excited contemplating his chance to prove himself. Some others stared into the foliage on the opposite bank and jabbered excitedly in whispers as their imaginations got the better of them,after which a strange silence set in as frightened eyes scanned the environment. For long passing minutes they could hear each other breathe. No one broke the self-imposed silence. They at least tried their best to be as quiet as possible under the circumstances.

"I assure you I don't like it as much as you don't, Mr Ellis. But we have to be patient. They may not be around anywhere here for all I, or for all you, for that matter, know."

Ellis stared into his face. "Didn't you send out any scouting details? It's preposterous," he exploded.

All he got from the taciturn Stirling was a superior sniff as he tried to ignore this show of what he regarded as childish petulance. His upper lips curled in a sneer. These civilians! All experts! He and Captain Irwin exchanged superior smiles. Irwin looked back at Ellis in a an aggressive manner.

The soldier, Corporal Heffron, who was farthest from Stirling suddenly pointed to something he had seen moving on the opposite bank as he shouted, "Over there, sir! Amongst the gum trees, sir."

That caused a flutter and surge of movement. Captain Irwin ordered his sergeant to take two riders and investigate the sighting. Sergeant Watts and two others rode off and spoke urgently to the red-headed settler. A lot of finger-pointing ensued and urgent exchanges of ideas but at the end of it the sergeant and his men rode back to Irwin, their senior commander, and reported that nothing definite had emerged. Perhaps some excitement and anxieties had gone towards creating the settler's imagined sightings. At this stage that was all it seemed to be. Irwin nodded his thanks and rode down to the river bank for another look. He wasn't the man to let others make up his mind, being obdurate and a forceful leader of men.

Suddenly the silence of the river plain was shattered by a hellish outbreak of strange calls. It sounded like a pack of wild animal calls the natives usually made before they attacked. It was more like some strange sort of barking. From a distance the settlers heard didgeridoos from one end of the river bank which was echoed later by similar sounds from the opposite end. From end to end this was repeated. It played on the nerves of the white men. They grasped their rifles tightly and searched the river gums with straining and anxious eyes. The mounted men drew their sabers and alerted their mounts preparatory to going into action.

Time passed slowly as Captain Irwin waited to see an enemy to engage in assault but the native warriors were too well camouflaged behind the trees and bushes. Their tactics were acknowledged by Governor Stirling as he rode his animal closer to Captain Irwin who whispered a command in the ear of a junior officer who was closest to him. The officer rode up to a settler hiding behind a bush. The two remained in conference for a few moments till the man,one George Timothy Smith, a former convict but reformed and now in the employ of a farmer,broke cover and went out into the river which he proceeded to wade till he was waist deep. Suddenly a spear flew over the surface of the water and then went through the man's body,killing him instantly.

From the midst of the settlers a fusillade replied as they fired into the bushes. Nothing happened. The aborigines were disciplined and played a waiting game.

"Hold your fire!" ordered Irwin realizing they were wasting ammunition. They could not hope to hit anything they could not see. The party were obviously very nervous. He didn't want them to break out into a panic that would only weaken them and give the advantage to the indigenous warriors. He ordered a formation of a phalanx of those from the 21st Regiment who were there that day to face the enemy. Bushes and trees began to move frenetically all at once. It looked like a jungle coming alive and behaving aggressively. The soldiers fell back. From their hidden vantage points the warriors hurled spears which hit nothing. The sergeant rode up to confer with his leader, Capt Frederick Irwin. They concurred to wait for the next volley and when it came to fire at the closest and nearest spear cluster. They waited and waited. The men were clearly nervous and held fingers on triggers. Whispers ran their round in tones of stress and fear. Calyute played the game with cunning and precision.

The sergeant tried to keep his voice calm as he ordered them when the time came to return fire at the nearest cluster and then charge the enemy, swordsmen to the fore of the retaliation. They didn't have to wait much longer. Ear-splitting cries filled the air. From several places of concealment spears floated silently in deadly formation into their midst. The afternoon air was rent with the screams of the wounded, the war cries of the warriors matched the volume of threats and taunts of the settlers, and the cries of terrified horses. Rifles opened fire immediately as the order rent the air, "Fire!"

Those settlers who were armed with sabres splashed across the river with blood curdling yells. This took the native warriors by surprise who abandoned their positions and fled. They lacked any second line of defensive tactics. That wasn't how they fought. Calyute's defense had wilted suddenly.

Lester Yeo, formerly a forger who had done time in Van Diemen's Land and come over to the Swan River Colony looking for a new life, confronted a warrior who yelled a challenge at him. It was the last thing he did because the settler very nearly slashed his head off. The warrior fell spraying a fountain of blood. An older native was much slower than the younger warriors and subsequently was run through by Yeo's weapon and fell into the river in his death throes, flailing at the waters till he was swept down by the waves of the river.

It later transpired that the native force came to be split as the mere handful Whadjuk who were really not all that keen warriors withdrew from the river and retreated some way from the battle by the river whilst Calyute marshalled his brave Bindjareb people for a last stand alone. He swore he would take revenge on the cowardly Whadjuk later if he lived. They would not be allowed to share the fruits of Mandjoogoordup, traditional Bindjareb land.

In a reckless act he killed a settler and grabbed his sword off him after he fell. He flailed wildly at the horses and anyone near enough to kill. Yeo did not realize that Calyute was behind him. But instinctively he turned to meet an enemy but it was too late. Calyute hacked at him many times almost dismembering him. Police Superintendent T.T Ellis saw what had happened to Yeo so he spurred his horse in that direction with his sabre thrust before him. Two painted Bindjareb warriors launched their spears at him.

One went clean through his shoulder and the other lodged in his right temple, and the police superintend fell dead.

Just before the going down of the sun the police action was concluded. Some

warriors finding themselves overcome by a superior fire power retreated, taking with them women and children hidden a short distance from the battle, using the native trees and bushes expertly and thus saved many of them. The less fortunate fell as they fled.

Once clear from the river they paused in flight and looked about for Calyute, but there was no sign of him. They asked each other for any news about their chief. No one saw him die so they presumed the worst, that he had been captured by the white men.

On the other side Sergeant Meares called off the action and ordered the settlers to the shore to tend to the wounded. He sent a party from his 21st Regiment to explore the opposite shore from where the Bindjareb had sprung their ambush. The party of settlers took a count of the wounded and the dead.

The sergeant called out to Captain Irwin, "Over here,sir." and when Irwin rode up to him the sergeant pointed out something to him. "All shot in the back,sir," he said with a distasteful grimace.

"Not a word, you understand,sergeant? Not a word to anyone. What's your name?"

"William Meares,sir."

"Good, Sergeant Meares. This is only between you and me. Understand? If it leaks out you are a dead man,"Irwin grated between his teeth."Not a word, Meares, not to anyone!" Then he rode away to oversee to the recovery process. There were wounded horses in a distressed state. They needed care.

Those who were too badly wounded were shot to ease them of their pain and to make it unnecessary to give them the extra care that would have been needed,the care they weren't equipped to give them. In the circumstances it was the most humane thing that could have been done.

A thick mist had rolled in through the forest. It brought in cold air from the ocean. It was somewhat strange for the month of October, but then there had been strange weather patterns that had been taking place and made life a bit difficult to cope with. Thus the Battle of Pinjarra began and ended, a mere oddity in the annals of early Australian history, particularly of that part of a remote Western Australia, a tract of land hardly worth the attention of the arrogant colonists in the east.

Here, by the banks of the Murray, the ghost gums that lined the banks of the river, lived up to their name, infused by the spirits of those who had been felled in battle and their women and children, or so it seemed to the native warrior people. They covered themselves with the low-lying and smothering white mists making it difficult for the settlers to see through but giving the battered remains of just half of the eighty or so natives a chance to escape, pursued now and then by the last angry shot or two of panicky soldiers of the 21st Regiment who imagined they were still seeing a hidden enemy near them somewhere in the thickets and behind the ghost gums.

The prisoners were bound hand and foot. The prize amongst these hapless prisoners were Monang, Yeyong and their leader, Calyute. They were closely watched as they made their way eastward to the colony of Mandurah that Peel had taken so much trouble setting up. Once there, they were locked up in a single cell in what passed for the police station. There they were fed and washed and given water to drink. All the while three posts were being driven into a sand strip facing the ocean. They worked on the erections for a whole day. In that time the prisoners were visited by a magistrate who spoke to them but doubted that the prisoners understood much of what was said. He ordered the men to be produced before his court on Monday, the week-end coming in between. What followed was a shambles as far as traditional military proceedings were concerned as few of the settlers understood legal procedure but this didn't prevent the court room being jammed by the many who turned out to see justice done. This meant hearing the sentence that was a foregone conclusion. Monang and Yeyong were to be taken out to the estuary where the whipping posts hastily erected waited for the sentences to be administered, where each to receive ten lashes whilst their leader, Calyute, would get twenty, then taken out beyond the limits of the settlements and released into the wilds where it was assumed they should be fully capable of tending their own wounds and foraging for their own food. Their people would soon enough find them and take care of them.

Monday arrived wild and windy, cloud cover increasing. The settlers, men, women and children, created somewhat of a picnic atmosphere with picnic baskets and blankets for ground cover complete. Children played catch-ee games, ironically enough.

A crude attempt at official procedure was followed and two burly soldiers flexed their muscles and circled the three who were bound to the remains of tree trunks and practiced with their whips which made whistling sounds in the air. At a command from Captain Irwin two soldiers measured off the distances to their targets and brought down their whips with an awful sickening sound of tearing flesh. Monang and Yeyong were young and their youth unacquainted with such barbaric sentences against guilty offenders. The whistling and tearing sounds mingled with their cries and a moaning of the winds blowing in and driving dark clouds from across the ocean. Their ravaged bodies twitched and shuddered. At the same time groups of children ran about the beach for vantage points to witness what they found exciting. They whooped and waved their hands about, some chased by parents whose tempers frayed at their embarrassing show of enthusiasm for the punishing lashes. They eluded every attempt of parents and others to chase them away from being witness to such brutality. To the children it was too much fun on which to miss out.

Gulls rose and became entangled in thermal currents in the air and cried out in anger at such intrusions which contrasted sickeningly with the usual sounds of a gentler and accustomed settlement life. Then came the main event, attention given to Calyute who looked into the eyes of Capt. Irwin unflinchingly even as the whip lashed him mercilessly. The native chief gritted his teeth but would not let even a moan escape for the satisfaction of those who hated him. Lashings were marked by growing rivulets of blood in a geography of inhumanity. His body broke out in involuntary twitches with the pain.

Back at the scene of the massacre, the Murray still flowed serenely as if it had noticed nothing abhorrent. It flowed without a sense of its history that was fated to be hidden away and not acknowledged, caught like a guilty thing in its musty concealment of poorly and inadequately written accounts, in other words, the sordid lies of lying chroniclers. After all,it is the victor who writes the history and offers the world the truth,isn't it ?

From under bushy thickets and giant ferns crept a lonely figure who had managed to escape the attention of the victors, who had witnessed the obscene actions of the settlers and the authority they labored under,who crept about like an furtive animal, still bloodied but not substantially or critically wounded. He shivered in fear and pain and peered about nervously. It wasn't the physical pain that numbed his conscious life now but the ghastly memories of how his wife,mother and their two young children died in the hail of bullets that mowed them down indiscriminately as they tried to flee the carnage. He painfully visited each spot he saw one or the other fall. He found burial spots where, with body and mind aching, he laid each in the graves he managed to claw out and bury them in the bloodied earth and covered each up,. He looked about at where other corpses had fallen. He knew most of them. He noted that nowhere could he find Calyute. It was the only little victory he weakly celebrated. He lay down exhausted,drifting in and out of consciousness wishing for a death of his own.

That was how the Rev John Webb found him. From afar,he had heard the sound of the firing, he had heard the screams and cries of battle from a place of concealment, unable to do anything to stop the bloody proceedings. Now he emerged and approached the prone,lifeless warriors. He wasn't afraid for himself as much as he feared he was witnessing genocide. He would be committed to positive, moral action. It would pit him against the establishment that already was most unsympathetic to his ministry and the building of his little wattle and clay church on the edge of Peel's new settlement, Mandurah, that was slowly growing in size. He would be bereft of his mission if he made them confront their barbaric and sinful actions. He could even lose his life. The very prospect made him shiver.

It took a long time to calm the native warrior who trembled at the sight of another white man he both feared and hated and wanted to kill before he killed him. The standoff took all of what was left of the day. By patient ministration of giving him water and rum to drink and gently spreading salve over the wounds did the old priest slowly win over the hostility and enmity he encountered. They limped into the bush on the outskirts of the settlement. Rev Webb concealed him. He made up a bed on the earth and covered him with a blanket. The rain was setting in again. What he saw gave the old man hope of the native recovering but it would take much longer for the mental scars to be completely cured, if ever.

He had never met Calyute but from Jim Jam,whom he called his guest, he got a picture of the chieftain. He knew what he had to do. If he was alive he had to be found and helped to escape to wherever Calyute wanted to go. Rev Webb left the church and went about the search as unobtrusively as he could. He felt his image of a wild and mad creature in the settlement would be his best camouflage. He would return to his church by nightfall with bread and some fruit for Jim Jam, who had made good progress physically, but would startle suddenly at any harmless little sound from the outside of the hut.

Soon after, on a dark and moonless night, he accidentally discovered Calyute. He was passing the trading store when he could make out the shadowy figures of three men who ran from one shelter to another till they got to the edge of the settlement where they made a dash into the bush and were soon swallowed up by the dense vegetation that surrounded Mandurah.

The morning after the escape there was great anxiety at the lack of proper security. Those who were entrusted with guarding against any breakout were severely reprimanded and officials were sacked. The officer in charge of the detail, Sergeant Meares was demoted. Many rumors were spread as to how the escape had been successfully perpetrated. For a while it was the talking point in Mandurah, Fremantle and throughout the Swan Valley. The settlers were asked to be doubly vigilant and to report any sightings of the escapees. A big reward for the recapture of the three native warriors was posted in every public facility.

Rev Webb and his faithful Jim Jam wandered the bushland nearby and even beyond hoping to be the first to find the trio but without success. They feared for their well-being should the soldiers and police get to them before anyone else did. They concluded that the warriors must have fled farther afield, perhaps to the Swan Valley where there were (some) some few Bindjareb people who managed to share the hunting rights with the Noongar people with whom there had been a degree of inter-tribal marriage and accommodation of tribal culture.

However, Calyute and his friends, Monang and Yeoyong, lived a separate existence on the foothills of the escarpment. The Pinjarra massacre had been put aside, but not forgotten. They never forgot nor forgave the white settlers but remembered the kindness of the old man who had been so helpful to them and cared for them. They could not understand why he had been so different. They thought he must have been mad.

They returned to an idyllic life of the noble brave. They made new spears and tested them and worked hard to perfect their balance and effectiveness. They were successful in securing three each for their daily needs. Some were made to spear fish and others that were heavier were to spear kangaroos,and any other animals known to be edible. Their nearness to nature made them happier and feel fulfilled. They decided that this was how they really wished to live in future. They could do nothing to expel the white strangers who looked as if they were now permanent settlers. They could not be driven from the valley.Maybe there may come a time later when all the black warriors would be able to unite under strong chieftains and kill them all. But that would come many years from the present. Maybe Yagan was right in the end.

They would return to Moodjoogoorup and find wives to share their lives and bear them children. They accordingly built mia mias close to the Murray River once again, but only in the upper reaches of the river where the undergrowth was denser. This was only when they felt secure there. They met others of their tribe and went to the coroborees and hunting for animals. The other Bindjareb were only too happy to meet them once more. The young bucks were particularly friendly with Yeoyong and Monang. Calyute had acquired iconic stature. However he rejected any honors they wanted to bestow on him. He often broke away to wander by himself. For hours he would sit by himself staring into the bush or up river. Often he sat motionless following the aerial movement of birds on thermal currents. He was one with all of them. The tribe had come to appreciate his love for solitude. He was deemed to have the powers of a shaman.

Calyute took Monang with him one day as they entered Noongar territory. They had secretly planned to get help from any neighbouring people and develop a force to make one more attempt to drive the white people back into their ships and force them back to the lands of the clouds from where they had come. They met with the great warriors of the Swan valley, Yagan and another warrior, Gyallipert, but try as hard as they did they could not get them to form a coalition against the white devils. The Noongars were too concerned with their life and to protect their fishing and hunting rights.

Yagan was sympathetic but felt the time was not come as yet to rise against the white devils. He had spoken to other chiefs but had got little or no support from the Swan Valley tribes. They preferred to live amicably with the British settlers. Somehow word leaked out to the whites about the presence of Calyute and his son Monang and what they were trying to do. Troops of armed police rode the countryside looking for them to take them in but they couldn't find them anywhere. The pair had run away to their own lands where they would never again be found.

Word would come down to them when, from places of concealment, parties of white men could be seen. The progress that had been made in their relationships with the foreigners was now forever damaged. The white men were now clearly the enemies who had to be avoided and, to some young hot blood, killed whenever it was safe to do so. They had started a campaign of stealing and burning properties. They were hunted down and killed from time to time. The elders no longer were able to exert control over their depredations. They, at best, now enjoyed a very tenuous hold on life and even less on their history in what had once been their tribal lands which now wilted under occupancy. Theirs was a destiny that had become mortgaged to servitude as they became transformed in biblical proportions as hewers of wood and drawers of water for the foreigners.

The natives understood their responsibilities to their environment. Their stewardship was learned through the traditional lessons to preserve the environment by burning off parts of the bush so that new trees and shrubs would replace the old and dying plants. In this process some outlying farms had been burnt. The devastated settlers reported seeing natives running with flaming branches to destroy their properties. Roe and Sterling understood that this was part of the native campaign of annual warring provocations and they had to be taught a lesson once and for all. The punishment at Pinjarra hadn't deterred them in their counter-attacks. They mustered as big a force of armed men to carry out a punishment that had the dimension of a genocide.

The tribal warriors of the Bindjareb became aware of this plan and duly withdrew to the southern reaches of the escarpment as far as they could get from Mandurah. They looked for Calyute whose absence these last few days had been alarming over his health and well-being. Monang and Yeoyong thought they could find him so they went off on their own to the banks of the Murray. Eventually they came across the inert and prone form of Calyute. They called to him but got no response. They ran down as a matter of some urgency and approached him calling his name but there was no response. They finally got to him and stood over his body and stood silently. Both warriors looked at each other, their alarm growing every moment. As one they dropped to their knees and rolled him over.

Calyute was dead.

He had died in his sleep, his clenched right fist on his chest.

A cold fear tore through their hearts. They feared for Calyute; they feared for their people.

He had become accepted as their chief, as their last chief. Where are the Bindjareb today? Whilst he lived he had been their protector. His was the spirit that was one with the land. After his passing they were alone and vulnerable and they felt this loss deeply. They ran back to the waiting people. A wailing ran through the bush. They wasted no time in leaving Mandjoogoorup . There was no knowing when or if they would ever return. A party of braves went back to carry Calyute whose remains would rest where no one ever found in the years that followed.

Stirling and Roe abandoned their search for who they believed were the belligerent marauding miscreants,believing that they had frightened them off. Stirling would have preferred killing them off as a permanent solution. The settlers would then on be safe from them and the settlement would grow and flourish as time went by. More villages and towns and joining roads would follow. A new history was being written, their history. They would do their duty to the natives by bringing them hospitals and medicines,education and a modern and superior life. No one asked the indigent races what they wanted, whether they wanted this or not. Those who survive and prevail are the ones who get to write history.

A new history would have needed the testimony of men like Rev John Webb and his friend, Jim Jam, if ever asked for or admitted in the letters and annals of the settlement that came into being.

Rev Webb passed away shortly after the massacre at Pinjarra. No one ever saw Jim Jam again;no one knew where he went. Before they dropped out of history one way or the other they both had appeared before the top most inquiry at Fremantle. Lord Slattery of Cambridgeshire was passing through having fulfilled his contractual duties in Melbourne and was to spend a few weeks in the new Swan Valley settlement and the neighboring settlements and present a report to Her Majesty,Queen Victoria,in England.

As had been expected the inquiry could only have gone one way. The murderous and thieving natives were increasing in their lawlessness and were a menace to the developing colony in western Australia. At Pinjarra on the banks of the Murray River they ambushed the legal party that was investigating the unfortunate incident. They had to defend themselves and in the process a number of natives died and they lost Mr Ellis unfortunately. Before the court of inquiry concluded and rose to retire, therefore, an old man and a native made their appearance before the board and asked to be heard. Before the authorities of the settlements could deny the request Lord Slattery, who was clearly intrigued, asked to hear what Rev Webb had to say, but it was to be off the record.

In quavering voice Rev Webb, who attended the court hearing, said that what happened that day had to go to the history of the west in time to come. He doubted all the facts would not. They would be carefully edited out. It caused a political furore. This led to the walkout of most of the court except Governor Stirling. Rev Webb was abused and heckled by most of the settlers.

Before he died Rev Webb had spoken of the first sighting of the white settlers by the aborigines of the Swan Valley who later said that they thought they were seeing their ancestors whose resurrected bodies were to be worshiped, or at the very least, to be highly respected. Accordingly the tribes were anxious to extend every generosity and accord and every respect to them. This led to a subservient attitude which was taken advantage of by those who failed to understand the due deference. They treated the aborigines as slaves, something the aborigines began to resent. They were a proud race and wouldn't tolerate any abasement. This led to trouble.

The natives quite logically argued that the whites fished in their rivers and the ocean and availed themselves of the resources of their land. In addition they shot their wild fowl and kangaroos for fresh meat. The aborigines thought they could reciprocate by spearing and stealing their cattle and sheep. They obviously thought this was only fair. For this they were sorely punished by beatings and incarcerations. When the settlers sowed and harvested wheat they took the wheat to a mill that Shenton and his men had constructed. There they used the grain to make flour. The natives soon learned all about bread and how it was made. They thought they were entitled to some of the proceeds so one day some braves raided Shenton's Mill and made off with some bags of wheat. They were regarded from then on as a nation of thieves who were not to be allowed in the settlement. Outlying farms were allowed to store firearms to defend themselves against the thieving natives. This set one race against the other. Thus an " us" and "them" mentality was born and later formed the basis of racial discrimination. Whatever was to be gained from the earth belonged to the colonial culture and the aborigines became the subordinate nation within the dominant nation.

History has a way of reflecting the will and accounts of the victorious and what came to be the established dominant culture.

Printed in the United States
By Bookmasters